Madrigals

Madrid Tales

Stories selected
and translated by

Margaret Jull Costa

Edited by

Helen Constantine

OXFORD
UNIVERSITY PRESS

OXFORD

UNIVERSITY PRESS

Great Clarendon Street, Oxford OX2 6DP

Oxford University Press is a department of the University of Oxford.
It furthers the University's objective of excellence in research, scholarship,
and education by publishing worldwide in

Oxford New York

Auckland Cape Town Dar es Salaam Hong Kong Karachi
Kuala Lumpur Madrid Melbourne Mexico City Nairobi
New Delhi Shanghai Taipei Toronto

With offices in

Argentina Austria Brazil Chile Czech Republic France Greece
Guatemala Hungary Italy Japan Poland Portugal Singapore
South Korea Switzerland Thailand Turkey Ukraine Vietnam

Oxford is a registered trade mark of Oxford University Press
in the UK and in certain other countries

Published in the United States
by Oxford University Press Inc., New York

British Library Cataloguing in Publication Data

Data available

Library of Congress Cataloging in Publication Data

Library of Congress Control Number: 2011941286

Typeset by SPI Publisher Services, Pondicherry, India
Printed in Great Britain
on acid-free paper by
Clays Ltd, St Ives plc

ISBN 978-0-19-958327-0

1 3 5 7 9 10 8 6 4 2

Contents

General Introduction   1

Introduction   7

The Novel on the Tram
Benito Pérez Galdós   15

The Solution
Emilia Pardo Bazán   53

Sunday Morning
Alonso Zamora Vicente   61

A Testing Time
Juan García Hortelano   67

Murder at the Atlantic
Guillermo Busutil   91

Luzmila
Álvaro Pombo   99

The Ballad of the River Manzanares
Ignacio Aldecoa   121

vi ■ Contents

A Clear Conscience
Carmen Martín Gaite   131

Restless Eyes
Medardo Fraile   155

**Mozart, K. 124, for Flute
and Orchestra**
Jorge Ferrer-Vidal   167

Through the Wall
Marina Mayoral   177

Return Journey
Carlos Castán   189

Flying Fish
Eloy Tizón   203

Let the Passengers Out
José Ferrer-Bermejo   209

Fallen from Fortune
Javier Marías   219

Personality Disorders
Juan José Millás   243

How can this be happening to me?
Carmen Posadas   255

Manolito's Toggle
Elvira Lindo   267

Sign and Message
José María Merino   281

Notes on the Authors   300

Further Reading   307

Publisher's Acknowledgements   312

Map of Madrid   314

Metro Map   316

Picture Credits

Page 14: © Bettmann/Corbis

Page 52: © Eric Isselée/Fotolia.com

Page 60: © Susana Vera/Reuters/Corbis

Page 66: © Rue des Archives/Tallandier/Mary Evans Picture Library

Page 90: © Creasource/Corbis

Page 98: © LOOK-foto/Wildcard Images, UK

Pages 120, 154, 188: © Alexander Stübner

Page 130: © Friedrich/Interfoto/Mary Evans

Page 166: © Owen Franken/Corbis

Page 176: © Stefano Costantini, flickr.com/stefanocostantini

Page 202: © Dmitrij/Fotolia.com

Page 208: © Jose Manuel Mazintosh

Page 218: © CSLD/iStockphoto

Page 242: © Michaela Steininger/Shutterstock

Page 254: © Image Source/Corbis

Page 266: © Gianni Ferrari/Cover/Getty Images

Page 280: © PjrTravel/Alamy

Page 314 (coat of arms): © Atlaspix/Shutterstock.com

Page 316: © Metro de Madrid, 2011. All rights reserved

General Introduction

The public face of the capital of Spain, let alone its less public face, may not be as instantly recognizable as that of, say, Paris or Rome, but it is just as captivating. The stories set amongst its streets and cafés, metro and parks, chosen and translated here by Margaret Jull Costa, reflect the character of the city and the lives of the *madrileños*, as its inhabitants are called, from the nineteenth century to the present day. We encounter stories that reflect 'all types, halfwits and very sharp minds, the very rich and the very poor', as the hero of a seventeenth-century picaresque novel by Quevedo is told. These stories reveal to us the lives of its poorest inhabitants and of the comfortable middle classes.

It is often said that stories and novels reflect 'a spirit of place', but we might ask what we mean by that. Madrid in 1561, before the Spanish court moved from Toledo, was a hill town, originally Arab, of not more than 30,000 inhabitants. Today it has taken its place in Europe as a buzzing, exciting administrative, cultural, and commercial centre.

So what is the spirit of that place, that changing city, and how can we define it?

Part of the fascination exerted by any large city is this: a city has many 'spirits' within it and one part rarely has the same feel or atmosphere as another. The division of Madrid into twenty-one *barrios*, a word which occurs frequently throughout this book, resembles the division of Paris into *arrondissements*, and to some extent the *rioni* in Rome, each with its particular character. In *Paris Tales* the stories are based precisely in those districts, in *French Tales* each one comes from a specific region, and in *Paris Metro Tales* the stories are related to the metro stations; but in *Madrid Tales* there is a perpetual moving from one *barrio* into another, like a fast-moving film, which gives a true and vivid picture of this bustling city constantly on the move, in the daytime, but perhaps more especially at night.

During Franco's regime, after the 1960s, the south-east of the city became more and more industrialized as the rural population migrated from the country and a slum settlement grew up in that area. Several stories, such as 'The Ballad of the River Manzanares', illustrate the poverty of working-class lives in this district, but we travel from there to a plusher district in the north of the city, where the luxurious apartments inhabited by Abel, the sun-worshipper, or by the otherwise unfortunate Lola are located. And that setting contrasts again with the gentility of the Buen Retiro gardens with their flavour of the Belle Époque—cultivated in imitation of the French style—where Frasquita walks her dog Mosquito in 'The Solution'.

In this anthology the reader has a real sense of travelling through the city. Some stories are bizarre, some funny, some serious, but as we read, the famous streets and monuments of Madrid—Cibeles, Calle de Alcalá, Plaza Mayor, the Palacio Real—pass before our eyes like a moving picture. What strikes us is the constant movement, from one area to another but also within the stories themselves. In 'A Clear Conscience', the doctor, whose lifestyle is very much that of the well-to-do and self-aware middle class, has to drive to one of the poorer *barrios* of Madrid, Puente de Vallecas, to tend a dying child. There, alongside the dirt track, he sees a dog standing on a pile of rubbish. In 'Fallen from Fortune', it is a trip to the airport by taxi that looms horribly large. In 'Let the Passengers Out', the passenger, in a dream-like state of panic, is desperately searching for a way out of the station. And Galdós, possibly Spain's best-known writer after Cervantes, takes the image of the tram, in particular one of the first double-decker trams of the sort introduced in Madrid towards the end of the nineteenth century, as a 'miniature world of passions', and weaves his clever and amusing story around that image.

A sense of place, as we all know, surfaces most palpably in childhood memories, often the most vivid in a person's life, and readers will find several examples in this book as in the other volumes in this series. In *Berlin Tales*, for instance, there were the stories by Julia Franck and Monika Maron; among the French tales, texts by Colette and Perec. In *Madrid Tales*, 'Flying Fish' by Eloy Tizón, in which the river Manzanares plays a key role, and 'Manolito's Toggle' by Elvira Lindo, set in the working-class district of Carabanchel where there were 'no famous people and no toggles', brilliantly recall the writers' experience of childhood. Schooldays and adolescence, as in the companion volumes, also figure very clearly in wry stories by Castán and Ferrer-Vidal. 'A Testing Time', by Hortelano, illustrates the uncertainties of adolescence and the political divisions that split Spain during and after the Civil War. As with the other volumes in this series, perhaps especially the stories from Berlin and Rome, this collection reflects to some degree the socio-historical as well as the topographical background.

There is a map at the back of the book to indicate the places mentioned in the stories and photographs complement and accompany each story. The reader will also find there biographical notes on the authors and suggestions for further reading. This anthology is offered to real or armchair travellers in the hope that it will enhance their experience of visiting Madrid by showing them aspects of the city they would not otherwise see as tourists, and deepening their appreciation of its inhabitants through their stories. But, like all the other volumes, this one is a journey into the realms of literature; through the real city the traveller will gain access to a world of new and unfamiliar writing and to some wonderful fiction.

Introduction

I first went to Madrid in late September 1975 as a rather inexperienced English language assistant in a secondary school in the working-class district of Carabanchel. I lived in a top-floor apartment in Calle Mesón de Paredes—up several flights of dark, worn stairs—in Lavapies, an area where the tall buildings, grimy walls, narrow streets, and cheap bars and restaurants were redolent of the Galdós novels I so loved as an undergraduate. At night, if you arrived home late, you had to clap your hands to summon the *sereno*, the nightwatchman, to unlock the vast street door (Franco's Spain was nothing if not security-conscious). Two-and-a-half months after I arrived, Franco finally died, and there were queues around the block to view him in his coffin. Most people—so the joke went—were there simply to make quite sure that he really was dead. I remember turning on the radio that morning to hear only funeral music, then arriving at school to be told that there was no school that day. I remember the feeling of elation, the feeling that everything was about to change.

And it did. Elections were held in 1977, and in 1980, the openly gay director Pedro Almodóvar made the first of his eccentric, irreverently funny, and overtly sexual feature films, *Pepe, Luci, Bom y otras chicas del montón*—both of which would have been unimaginable under Franco's prim, repressive regime. Madrid became the capital of the *movida*, the name given to the social and cultural scene that developed in the late 1970s and early 80s, fuelled by writers, fashion designers, artists, and film-makers. Twenty-first-century Madrid is different again. Like most large European cities, it has a fairly large immigrant population, is blighted by traffic and the problems of unemployment, drugs, and a drinking culture among young people; however, it is still inescapably Madrid, and its inhabitants inescapably *madrileño*. And Madrid probably still has the most frenetic nightlife—lasting into the small hours—of any European capital city.

While the films of Almodóvar have done much to establish Madrid in the imaginations of cinema-goers (although his is, admittedly, a somewhat skewed vision), literary representations of Madrid are less well known to English language readers. Foreign visitors have been alternately repelled and entranced by the city. Richard Ford disliked it, Hemingway loved it. George Borrow, in the 1840s, wrote: 'I will not dwell upon its streets, its edifices, its public squares, its fountains, though some of these are remarkable enough ... But the population! Within a mud wall, scarcely one league and a half in circuit, are contained two hundred thousand human beings, certainly forming the most extraordinary vital mass to be found in the entire world; and be it always remembered that this mass is strictly Spanish!' The mud wall is long gone, the population is over three million and certainly not strictly Spanish, but Madrid's 'extraordinary vital mass' has continued to exercise the same fascination on Spanish writers.

The first of the authors in this anthology is Spain's greatest nineteenth-century novelist, Benito Pérez Galdós. He was born in the Canary Islands, but moved to Madrid to study law. Seduced, however, by the seething life of the city, he promptly abandoned law for literature; and the city and its denizens became the subject matter of his finest novels, notably his masterpiece, *Fortunata y Jacinta*. Like all the best Realist novelists, his novels and short stories often have a vein of fantasy in them (which is perhaps why the film-maker Luis Buñuel was so drawn to his work), and the story in this collection is no exception. 'The Novel on the Tram' (written in 1871 when the double-decker horse-drawn tram had just been introduced) is the ordinary man's nightmare and the novelist's dream, with stories emerging from every face, every gesture, every overheard conversation and snatch of newsprint. An apparently simple trip from one side of Madrid to the other—from the *barrio* of Salamanca to that of Pozas—leads the protagonist into arrant madness, and madness, I realize, is a theme in many of the stories in this collection. Is this, I wonder, a common response to urban life, a more specific response to living in Madrid, or is it something deep in the Spanish psyche that found its first fictional expression in Cervantes's *Don Quixote*? Here, madness seems to go hand in hand with the emotional and social isolation common to all large cities— even Madrid, that apparently most convivial and sociable of cities; the rumbustious life of bars and cafés is only a faint and insignificant echo to those locked in their own obsessions: the memory of a lost child in Marina Mayoral's 'Through the Wall', the world of wardrobes in Juan José Millás's 'Personality Disorders', secret signs in José María Merino's 'Sign and Message', communion wafers and the Baby Jesus in Álvaro Pombo's 'Luzmila'.

In any large city where social classes rub shoulders with each other, there are inevitably clashes and contrasts, and these are reflected in many of the stories. The rich, well-meaning doctor in Carmen Martín Gaite's 'A Clear Conscience' is helpless when faced by the abject poverty of the slum he visits; Luzmila, both as nanny and maid, is entirely invisible to the people she works for; the son of a wealthy family feels perfectly at liberty to grope the maid while she's doing the washing-up. The Madrid captured in this anthology contains all social classes, from the bickering courting couple in Ignacio Aldecoa's 'Ballad of the Manzanares' to the mismatched lower-middle-class husband and wife in Medardo Fraile's 'Restless Eyes'; from the leisured classes of nineteenth-century writer Emilia Pardo Bazán's 'The Solution' to the newly rich best-selling novelist in Carmen Posadas's 'How can this be happening to me?'; and Galdós's tram seems to contain almost every strata of society. I also wanted the stories to set before the reader as wide a variety of characters as possible—adolescent boys obsessed with sex; maids up from the country; provincial girls who slide into prostitution; a small boy excited at the prospect of going downtown with his grandfather; vain, self-absorbed 30-somethings with too much money; a scheming bisexual; immigrant families far from home; mafia types; diligent office-workers struggling to bring up a family.

Another rich vein is provided by stories written from a child's point of view. Guillermo Busutil, Elvira Lindo, and Eloy Tizón all shine a humorous light on the foibles and eccentricities of the adult world. Juan García Hortelano's 'A Testing Time', set in a Madrid where Franco's Nationalists are about to seize power, gives us a hormone-driven adolescent's view of the conflict, while Zamora Vicente, writing in 1985, takes a nostalgic look back at the Madrid of his childhood, evoking and mourning a state of innocence and wonder destroyed by the schism of war. The illusions of youth, meanwhile, are expertly evoked by Ferrer-Vidal and Carlos Castán, whose protagonists' misplaced nostalgia only leads them into further pain and humiliation.

A first priority in compiling this anthology was to find excellent stories that paint a vivid picture of Madrid life in all its facets—the buzzing life of bars, warm evenings by the Manzanares river, the subterranean terrors of the metro, Madrid's icy winters and hot, empty summers, student days in the sixties, the ruthless underworld of the city's mafia—but also to provide the reader with a kind of map of key places in Madrid—the Gran Vía, the Prado, the Retiro Park, the Plaza Mayor, and so on. These are places that most visitors to Madrid would visit, but the stories also take us into *barrios* unfrequented by tourists—poor, working-class areas like Carabanchel and Puente de Vallecas. Some, like the Galdós story and Carmen Martín Gaite's 'A Clear Conscience' take us on a journey across the city, while in Javier Marías's sinister tale, 'Fallen from Fortune', we accompany a couple unaware that their guide to all the usual tourist highlights is leading them to their death. In 'Through the Wall' and 'Personality Disorders', on the other hand, the characters barely leave their apartments, and the city lurks outside the windows—a place too alarming to visit.

As far as I know, none of these stories has previously been translated into English. Some names will be more familiar than others—Benito Pérez Galdós, Javier Marías, Juan José Millás, and Carmen Martín Gaite but all, I feel, deserve to be better known to an English-reading public.

My thanks go to my friend and colleague Annella McDermott (the translator of the José Ferrer-Bermejo story 'Let the Passengers Out'), who has been an indefatigable searcher-out and sifter of stories and without whom I would never have undertaken this project. I would also like to thank Helen Constantine for her enthusiasm and support, as well as Medardo Fraile, Carlos Castán, Karmelín Adams, and Ben Sherriff for all their help and advice.

Maps of the city and of the metro have been included to help readers track the various places mentioned and visited in the stories. *¡Buen viaje!*

The Novel on the Tram

Benito Pérez Galdós

I

The tram was setting off from one end of the *barrio* of Salamanca and heading across Madrid in the direction of Pozas. Gripped by the selfish desire to get a seat before all the other passengers—who, naturally, had precisely the same intention—I grabbed the handrail of the stairs leading to the upper deck, placed one foot on the platform, and climbed aboard, but at that very instant—I should have seen it coming!—I collided with another traveller entering from the other side. When I looked at him, I saw that he was my friend, Señor Dionisio Cascajares de la Vallina, a sensible, inoffensive fellow, who, on the occasion in question, was kind enough to greet me with an enthusiastic, heartfelt handshake.

Our unexpected collision had no major consequences, if you discount a slight dent inflicted on the straw hat perched on the head of an Englishwoman who was attempting to board the tram behind my friend and who, doubtless due to a lack of agility on her part, received a blow to her hat from his walking stick.

We sat down and, dismissing the incident as unimportant, started chatting.

Señor Dionisio Cascajares de la Vallina is a celebrated doctor—although his fame does not rest on his deep knowledge of pathology—and a thoroughly decent man, of whom no one has ever said that he was likely to steal other people's property or kill a fellow human being other than in the pursuit of his dangerous and scientific profession. It is true that the trust he inspires in a multitude of families from all strata of society has much to do with his pleasant manner and his indulgent way of giving his patients only the treatment they want, but it is also a well-known fact that, in his bounty, he provides other services too, always of a rigorously honest nature, but which have nothing to do with science.

He knows more interesting things about people's private lives than anyone else, and is an obsessive asker of questions, although he makes up for the vice of over-inquisitiveness by his equal readiness to tell you everything he knows about other people without your even having to ask. You can imagine then how eagerly the curious and the loose-tongued seek out the company of this fine example of human indiscretion.

This gentleman and friend—well, he's a friend to everyone—was the person sitting next to me as the tram slid smoothly over the rails down Calle de Serrano, stopping now and then to fill up the few remaining empty seats. Indeed, we were soon so crammed together that I was hard put to know what to do with the parcel of books I had with me, and which I placed first on one knee and then on the other. In the end, fearing that I might be bothering the English lady sitting to my left, I decided to perch on top of it.

II

'And where are you off to?' Cascajares asked, peering at me over his blue spectacles, which made me feel as if I were being scrutinized by two pairs of eyes.

I gave a somewhat evasive response, and he, doubtless not wishing to miss the opportunity of gleaning some useful snippet of information, asked further questions, along the lines of 'And what's So-and-so up to these days? And where's So-and-so living?' and other similar enquiries, none of which received very fulsome replies.

Finding each attempt at conversation blocked, he finally set off along the path best suited to his expansive temperament and began to blab.

'Poor Countess!' he said, shaking his head and adopting an expression of selfless compassion. 'If she had followed my advice, she wouldn't be in the appalling situation in which she finds herself now.'

'No, of course,' I replied mechanically, thus paying the Countess my own brief tribute of compassion.

'You see,' he went on, 'she has allowed herself to become completely dominated by that man, and he'll be master of the house one day. The poor thing thinks she can solve everything by weeping and wailing, but it's not true. She should act now, because the man's an out-and-out bounder and, I believe, capable of the most heinous of crimes.'

'Oh, yes, awful,' I said, unthinkingly sharing in his imaginings.

'It's the same with all men of evil instincts and low social status when they rise a little in the world. They become utterly insufferable. One look at his face will tell you that no good will come of him.'

'Absolutely. It stands out a mile.'

'Let me explain the situation to you briefly. The Countess is an excellent woman, angelic, as discreet as she is beautiful, and she really does deserve better luck.

However, she is married to a man who does not appreciate what a treasure he has and who devotes his life to gambling and all manner of other illicit pastimes. She, meanwhile, grows bored and weeps. Is it any surprise, then, that she should try to mask her sorrow by seeking honest entertainment elsewhere, wherever there's a piano? Indeed, I myself have told her as much. "Countess," I said, "life is too short, you need some diversion. In the end, the Count will repent of his folly, and your sorrows will be at an end." And I think I'm right.'

'Oh, I'm sure you are!' I said officiously, although I was as indifferent to the Countess's misfortunes then as I had been at the beginning.

'That's not the worst of it, though,' added Cascajares, striking the floor with his walking stick. 'Now the Count has got it into his head to be jealous, yes, of a certain young man who has undertaken to "amuse" the Countess.'

'It will be the envious husband's fault if he succeeds.'

'Now given that the Countess is virtue personified, none of this would matter, no, none of this would matter if there were not a dastardly fellow involved, who, I suspect, will bring disaster down upon the household.'

'Really? And who is this fellow?' I asked, my curiosity piqued.

'A former butler, of whom the Count is very fond, and who has set out to make that poor unhappy, sensitive lady suffer. It seems he is in possession of a compromising secret and with that weapon intends to … well, I don't know quite what exactly. It's disgraceful!'

'It certainly is and he deserves to be made an example of,' I said, joining him in unleashing my fury on the man.

'But *she* is innocent, *she* is an angel. Oh, but here we are at Cibeles already, yes, there's the Parque de Buenavista on the right. Stop the tram will you, my boy. I'm not one of those men who likes to jump off while the tram is moving and risk cracking my skull open on the paving stones. Goodbye, my friend, goodbye.'

The tram stopped and Don Dionisio Cascajares de la Vallina got off, having once more shaken my hand and caused a second dent in the English lady's hat, which had not yet recovered from the first assault.

III

I remained on the tram, and the odd thing is, I continued to think about that unknown Countess, about her cruel, suspicious consort, and, above all, about the sinister man who, to use the doctor's colourful turn of phrase, was about to bring disaster down upon the household. Consider, dear reader, the nature of the human mind: when Cascajares began telling me about those events, I found it irrelevant and boring, but it took scarcely a moment for my imagination to take up that same affair and turn it over and over in my mind, a psychological operation doubtless stimulated by the regular motion of the tram and the dull, monotonous sound of its wheels, grinding away at the iron rails.

In the end, though, I stopped thinking about what, in fact, held little real interest for me and, looking around the carriage, I began examining my fellow passengers carefully, one by one. Such different faces and such diverse expressions! Some seemed quite indifferent to those sitting next to them, while others reviewed the assembled crowd with impertinent curiosity; some were happy, others sad, one man was yawning, and another fellow further off was laughing; and despite the brevity of the journey, not a few were impatient for it to end; for there is nothing more annoying than being in the company of a dozen or so people all gazing at each other in silence and counting each other's wrinkles and moles and any other imperfections on face or clothing.

It's strange, that brief meeting with people we have never seen before and whom we will probably never see again. When we get on the tram, someone else is usually already there; others get on afterwards; some get off, leaving us alone, and then, finally, we get off too. It's an image of human life, in which being born and dying are like those entrances and exits I've described, and which, as the generations of travellers come and go, are constantly renewing the small world of the tram. They enter and leave, they are born and die. How many have been here before us! How many will come afterwards!

And to make the resemblance more complete, a tram contains a miniature world of passions. We judge many of those we see there to be excellent people, we like their looks and are even saddened when they leave. Then there are others who, on the contrary, we loathe on sight: we hate them for ten minutes, rather rancorously examine their phrenological character, and feel real pleasure when they leave. And meanwhile, the tram, that imitation of human life, keeps moving, constantly receiving and letting go, uniform, tireless, majestic, indifferent to what is going on inside, entirely unstirred by the barely repressed emotions of that dumbshow, always travelling along those two endless parallel steel lines, as long and slippery as the centuries.

IV

I remained immersed in this ocean of unsettling thoughts as the tram continued up Calle de Alcalá, until I was snatched from them by the sound of my parcel of books hitting the floor. I immediately picked the parcel up, and my eyes fell on the piece of newspaper that served as a wrapping for the books and so I idly read a line or two of print. My curiosity was immediately aroused. Certain names scattered over that scrap of newsprint caught both my eye and my memory. I searched for the beginning of the article, but could not find it. The paper was torn and, initially out of mere curiosity and subsequently with growing fascination, this is what I read:

The Countess was in a state of indescribable agitation. She was continually troubled by the presence of Mudarra, the insolent butler, who, forgetting his lowly origins, had dared to set his sights on her, a creature so far above him. The villain was constantly spying on her, watching her as one might watch one's prey. He was unconstrained by respect, and neither the sensibility nor the delicacy of that excellent lady proved an obstacle to his ignoble stalking of her."

Mudarra entered the Countess's bedroom late one night, and she, pale and agitated, and filled at once by shame and terror, lacked the courage to dismiss him.

'Do not be afraid, Countess,' he said with a forced, sinister smile that only increased the lady's anxiety. 'I have not come to harm you in any way.'

'Oh, dear God, when will this torment cease?' cried the Countess, letting one arm droop by her side in despair. 'Leave my room this instant, I cannot give in to your desires. How shameful to abuse both my weakness and the indifference of my husband, who is the sole author of my many misfortunes.'

'Why so upset, Countess?' asked the fearsome butler. 'If I did not hold the key to your perdition in my hand, if I could not divulge to the Count details regarding a certain young gentleman... but I will not make use of those terrible weapons. One day, you will understand when you see how selfless is the love I feel for you.'

When he said this, Mudarra took a few steps towards the Countess, who drew back from the monster in horror and repugnance."

Mudarra was a man of about fifty, dark, squat, and bowlegged, with a bristling brush of wiry hair, a large mouth, and prominent eye teeth. His eyes, half-hidden beneath his beetling black brows, were filled at that moment by the most bestial and urgent feelings of concupiscence.

'Ah, such coldness!' he exclaimed angrily, when he saw the lady's understandable indifference. 'If only I were a certain impeccably turned-out young man! Why so fastidious when you know I could easily tell the Count... And he would believe me, you can be sure of that; the Count has such confidence in me that anything I tell him he takes to be the gospel truth. And given how jealous he is, if I were to give him that little piece of paper...'

'You villain!' cried the Countess in a fit of noble indignation. 'I am innocent, and my husband would never give ear to such vile calumnies. And even if I were guilty, rather than buy my peace of mind at such a price, I would prefer a thousand times over to be despised by my husband and by everyone else. Get out of here this minute.'

'I have a temper too, Countess,' said the butler, swallowing his rage, 'yes, I, too, have a temper, and when thwarted ... But since you're being so unpleasant, let's continue in that vein. I know what I have to do now. I have been far too indulgent for far too long. For the last time, I ask that we be friends. Don't force me to do something foolish, Countess ...'

As he said this, Mudarra arranged his parchment-yellow skin and the stiff tendons of his face into something resembling a smile and advanced a few steps as if about to sit down on the sofa next to the Countess. She leapt to her feet, crying:

'Get out of here, you scoundrel! You know perfectly well I have no one to defend me! Get out of here!'

The butler was like a wild beast who has let slip the prey he had held for a moment in his claws. He snorted, made a threatening gesture, and then, very slowly and quietly, left the room. The Countess, trembling and breathless, cowering in a corner, listened as his footsteps gradually moved off, the sound muffled by the rugs in the next room. When she thought he had gone, she could finally breathe more easily.

She locked all the doors and tried to sleep, but sleep eluded her, her eyes still filled by the terrifying image of the monster.

'CHAPTER XI. The plot—When Mudarra left the Countess, he went straight to his own room and, in the grip of a terrible nervous disquiet, began leafing through various papers and letters, muttering: "I've had enough, she'll pay dearly for this ..." Then he sat down, took up his pen, and set before him one of those letters, which he studied closely before beginning another, trying to copy the handwriting. He kept glancing feverishly from one to the other, and at last, after much labour, he wrote the following letter—in a hand identical to that of the original: "I promised to see you, and I hasten ..."

The newspaper was torn at this point and I could read no more.

V

With my eyes still fixed on the parcel, I began thinking about the connection between what I had heard from Señor Cascajares de la Vallina and the scene I had just read about in that rag, a serial doubtless translated from some ridiculous novel by Ponson du Terrail or Montepin. I know it's nonsense, I said to myself, but the fact is she intrigues me, this Countess, this victim of the barbarous machinations of a ruthless butler, who only exists in the crazed mind of some novelist born to terrify simple folk.

How will the wretch take his revenge? He would be capable of anything, of the kind of atrocity dreamed up by such authors to conclude a particularly sensational chapter. And what will the Count do? And what about the young man mentioned first by Cascajares and later by Mudarra in the newspaper serial. What will he do? Who is he? What exactly is the relationship between that unknown gentleman and the Countess? I would love to know...

VI

I looked about me on the tram and, O horror, my eyes alighted on someone who made me tremble with fear. While I had been absorbed in reading that interesting fragment of serial, the tram had stopped several times to let off or take on the occasional passenger. One such passenger was the man whose sudden presence had so shaken me. It was him, Mudarra, the butler himself, sitting opposite me, his knees touching mine. In a moment, I had examined him from head to toe and recognized him from the description I had read. It could be none other; even the most insignificant details of his clothes clearly indicated it was him. I recognized his greasy, swarthy skin; the untameable hair growing in all directions, like the snakes on Medusa's head; the eyes almost concealed by his wild, bushy eyebrows; the pigeon toes; in short, the same look, the same man in appearance, attire, in the way he breathed and coughed, even in the way he put his hand in his pocket to pay his fare.

Then I saw him take out a wallet and noticed that this object bore a large gilt M, the initial of his surname. He opened the wallet, removed a letter, and studied the envelope with a demonic smile on his face. I could even imagine him muttering to himself:

'I've got her handwriting right off pat!'

It was, in fact, quite a short letter and the address on the envelope was written in a female hand. He looked at it hard, relishing his villainous handiwork, until he noticed that I, with indiscreet, discourteous curiosity, was peering over to read the address. He shot me a glance that struck me like a blow and immediately returned the letter to his wallet.

During the brief period of time it had taken me to read that fragment of a story, to ponder a little those strange events, and to find the unlikely, fantastical figure of Mudarra himself transformed into a living being and a fellow passenger on that journey, the tram had left behind it Calle de Alcalá, crossed Puerta del Sol, and emerged triumphant into Calle Mayor, pushing its way past the other carriages, scattering the slower, loitering carts, and frightening the pedestrians who, in the tumult of the street and dazed by the hubbub of noises, often failed to see the great hulk approaching until it was almost upon them.

I was still studying the man as one would an object of whose real existence one is not quite sure, and I did not take my eyes off his repellent features until I saw him stand up, call for the tram to stop, and get off, only to disappear at once among the crowds filling the street.

VII

Several people got on and off, and the living decor of the tram changed completely.

I was feeling increasingly curious about an event that, at first sight, could be seen as having been shaped exclusively by my own mind out of the disparate sensations occasioned by that initial conversation and by what I had read subsequently, but which I now imagined to be true and undoubtedly real.

When the man I believed to be the evil butler got off, I sat thinking about the letter and explained it to myself in my own fashion, not wishing, in such a delicate matter, to prove any less fertile in imagination than the novelist and author of the fragment I had read moments before. Mudarra, I thought, eager to avenge himself on the Countess—that poor unlucky Countess!—copies her handwriting and pens a letter to the young gentleman, with whom something may or may not have occurred. In the letter, she invites him to her house; the young man arrives at the appointed hour and, shortly afterwards, so does the husband, duly informed of the meeting, so that he can catch his unfaithful wife in flagrante. Very clever! Now while such a plan may have its pros and cons in real life, it works perfectly in a novel. The lady faints; the lover panics; the husband commits a terrible act; and behind the curtain lurks the fateful countenance of the butler, revelling in his devilish revenge.

I have read many novels, many of them very bad indeed, and it was I who gave that twist to a story that was silently evolving in my imagination on the flimsy basis of something a friend had told me, a few lines from a novel found on a scrap of newspaper, and an encounter on the tram with a complete stranger.

VIII

On and on the tram went, and whether because of the heat inside or because the slow, monotonous motion of the vehicle produces a kind of dizziness that can all too easily become sleep, the fact is, my eyelids began to droop, and as I listed slightly to the left, I leaned my elbow on my parcel of books and closed my eyes. However, I continued to see before me the row of faces, male and female, some bearded, others hairless, some laughing, some stiff and solemn. Then, it seemed to me that, as if at the command of a shared muscle, all those faces began to wink and grimace, opening and closing eyes and mouths and revealing a series of teeth that went from the purest of whites to the yellowest of yellows, some sharp and others blunt or worn. The eight noses that protruded from beneath those sixteen eyes of diverse colours and expression kept growing then shrinking, and constantly changing shape; the mouths opened horizontally, emitting silent guffaws, or else extended outwards to form long snouts, similar to the interesting face of a certain estimable animal whose name is anathema.

Through the window beyond those eight faces, whose horrific visages I have just described, I could see the street, the houses, and the passers-by, all moving very fast, as if the tram were travelling at vertiginous speed. To me, at least, it seemed to be going faster than any Spanish or French or English or American train; it was travelling as fast as you can possibly imagine a solid object moving through space.

As my lethargic state grew more pronounced, it seemed to me that the houses and streets and Madrid itself were disappearing. For a moment, I thought the tram was travelling through the depths of the sea; outside, I could see the bodies of vast whales and the sticky tendrils of a multitude of corals of various sizes. Small fish flicked their slippery tails against the glass and some peered in with large, golden eyes. Unfamiliar crustaceans, large molluscs, madrepores, sponges, and hordes of giant misshapen bivalves, of a kind I had never seen, passed ceaselessly by. The tram was being drawn by some sort of swimming monster, whose oars, pushing against the water, sounded like the beatings of a propeller that made the watery mass churn with its endless turning. This vision gradually faded and then it seemed to me that the tram was flying through the air, straight as a bullet, unbuffeted by the winds. There was nothing to be seen outside, only empty space; the clouds occasionally wrapped about us; a sudden, violent shower of rain drummed on the upper floor; then we emerged once more into pure sun-flooded space, only to plunge back into the vaporous bosom of immense cloudscapes—now red, now yellow, now the colour of opals, now of amethysts—which we left behind as we journeyed. At other times, we passed through a place filled by glowing masses of the finest gold dust; at still others, the dust, which I fancied came from the movement of the wheels grinding down the light, was first silver, then green like powdered emeralds, and finally, red like powdered rubies. The tram was being drawn now by some apocalyptic winged creature, stronger than a hippogryph and bolder than a dragon, and the sound of the wheels and the wings was reminiscent of the hum from the great sails of a windmill or from a bumblebee the size of an elephant. We flew through endless space, never arriving anywhere, and many leagues beneath our feet lay the Earth, and on the Earth was Spain, Madrid, the *barrio* of

Salamanca, Señor Cascajares, the Countess, the Count, Mudarra, and the unknown young man.

IX

I soon fell deeply asleep and then the tram stopped moving, stopped flying and I lost the feeling that I was travelling in a tram, and all that remained was the deep, monotonous rumble that never ceases during the nightmares that afflict one, be it in a train or in a cabin on board ship. I fell asleep. O unlucky Countess! I saw her as clearly as the piece of paper on which I am writing now; I saw her sitting at a table, resting her cheek on her hand, looking as sad and meditative as a statue representing melancholy. At her feet, a little dog lay curled, apparently as sad as his interesting mistress.

Then I was able to study at my leisure the woman I considered to be misfortune personified. She was tall and fair, with big, expressive eyes, a slender, almost large, but exquisitely shaped nose that stood out gracefully beneath the curve of her fine, blue-black eyebrows. She was simply coiffed, and from that and the way she was dressed, it was clear that she did not intend going out that night, that terrible, terrible night! With growing anxiety I watched the lovely face I so longed to know, and it seemed to me that I could read her thoughts on her noble brow, where the habit of mental concentration had traced a few imperceptible lines that time would transform into deep wrinkles.

X

Suddenly the door opened and in walked a man. The Countess gave a cry of surprise and sprang to her feet in a state of great agitation.

'What do you mean by this, Rafael?' she said. 'What impudence! Who let you in?'

'Were you not expecting me, Señora?', said the handsome young man, 'I received a letter from you ...'

'A letter from me!' the Countess exclaimed, in a state of still greater agitation. 'I wrote no such letter. Why would I?'

'But look, Señora,' said the young man, taking out the letter and showing it to her. 'It's in your own hand.'

'Dear God! What evil scheme is this?' she cried in despair. 'I did not write that letter. This is a trap that has been laid for me ...'

'Calm down, Señora ... And please forgive me.'

'Ah, I understand now. That vile man. I can guess what his idea was. You must leave at once. No, it's too late. I can hear my husband's voice.'

Indeed, a booming voice could be heard in the next room, and then the Count entered and, pretending to be surprised to find the young man there, he gave a rather affected laugh and said:

'Why, Rafael, fancy meeting you here. It's been such a long time. You came to keep Antonia company, I suppose. Well, do stay for tea.'

The Countess and her husband exchanged a dark look. In his confusion, the young man could barely manage to return the Count's greeting. I saw various servants come in and out; I saw them bring in the tea and then vanish, leaving the three main characters alone. Something terrible was about to happen.

They sat down. The Countess was as pale as death; the Count affected a wild hilarity, as if he were drunk; and the young man said nothing, answering only in monosyllables. Tea was poured, and the Count handed Rafael a cup, not any cup, but a particular one. The Countess stared at the cup with an expression of all-consuming horror on her face. They drank in silence, accompanying their tea with various tasty Huntley & Palmers biscuits and other titbits appropriate to the occasion. Then the Count gave another of those loud, crazy laughs peculiar to him that night and said:

'Well, this is dull! I can't get a word out of you, Rafael. Antonia, play something. It's been so long since we heard you. How about that piece by Gortzchach entitled *Death*? You used to play it so well. Come now, take your place at the piano.'

The Countess tried to speak, but could not utter a single word. Then her husband fixed her with his eyes, and she gave in, like a dove hypnotized by a boa constrictor. She got up and went over to the piano, and there the Count must have said something that terrified her still more, placing her in his infernal power. The piano spoke, a multitude of strings struck simultaneously; as the Countess's hands raced over the flats and sharps, they awoke in a second the hundreds of notes sleeping silently in the soundboard. At first, the music was a confusion of sounds that deafened rather than pleased, but then the storm abated, and a fearful, funereal song, like the *Dies Irae*, emerged from the disorder. I felt I could hear the sad singing of a choir of Carthusian monks, accompanied by the low moans of a bassoon. Then we heard mournful cries, as one imagines the cries of condemned souls in Purgatory to be, pleading incessantly for a forgiveness that will be long in coming.

Then it was back to those drawn-out, raucous arpeggios, notes jostling with each other, as if quarrelling over who should arrive first. The chords rose and fell just as the foam of the waves builds and is lost. The tune ebbed and flowed in an endless swell, dwindling almost to nothing, then returning with more force, forming great, churning eddies.

I was swept away by that powerful, majestic music. The Countess had her back to me and so I could not see her face, but I imagined that in her present state of bewilderment and fear, the piano must somehow be playing itself.

The young man was behind her, and the Count to her right, leaning on the piano. Occasionally, she glanced up at him, but she presumably found the expression in his eyes so terrifying that she immediately lowered her gaze and continued playing. Suddenly, the piano stopped, and the Countess screamed.

At that moment, I felt a hard blow on my shoulder that shook me violently awake.

XI

In the agitation of my dream, I had slid sideways and fallen on top of the venerable Englishwoman sitting next to me.

'You fell asleep on me!' she said, pulling a sour face and repelling the parcel of books that had fallen into her lap.

'Yes, Señora, you're quite right, I did fall asleep!' I answered, embarrassed to see how all the other passengers were laughing at me.

'I'm going to tell the conductor that you're bothering me. Shocking behaviour in a gentleman,' she added in her fractured Spanish. 'You seem to think that my body is a bed for you to sleep on. You are a stupid ass, sir!'

When she said these words, this daughter of Albion, who was already quite red in the face, turned bright scarlet. It looked as if the blood filling her cheeks and nose was about to burst forth from her glowing pores. She showed me four sharp, very white teeth, as if she were about to bite me. I begged her forgiveness for my discourteous behaviour while asleep, retrieved my parcel, and reviewed the new faces in the tram. Imagine my surprise, dear, patient, kindly reader, when I saw before me the young man from my dream, Don Rafael in person. I rubbed my eyes to convince myself I was not still sleeping, but I was definitely awake, as awake as I am now.

It was him, it really was, and he was talking to the man sitting next to him. I pricked up my ears and listened as if my life depended on it.

'But didn't you suspect anything?' the other man was saying.

'Yes, but I said nothing. She seemed half-dead with fear. Her husband ordered her to play the piano and she didn't dare refuse. As usual, she played admirably, and as I listened, I almost forgot about the dangerous situation we were in. Despite all her efforts to appear calm, there came a point when she could pretend no longer. Her arms grew limp, her fingers slipped from the keys, she threw back her head and cried out. Then her husband unsheathed a dagger and shouted furiously: "Play or I'll kill you!" When I saw this, my blood boiled. I went to throw myself on the wretch, but I had a feeling in my body I can't even describe. It was as if, suddenly, a bonfire had been lit in my stomach; fire was running through my veins; my temples were pounding, and I fell to the floor, unconscious.'

'Had you noticed no effects from the poison before?' asked the other man.

'I'd felt slightly unwell and had some vague suspicion that something was wrong, but that was all. The poison had been carefully prepared, because it took effect slowly and, while it didn't kill me, it left me with a condition that will stay with me for the rest of my life.'

'And after you lost consciousness, what happened then?'

Rafael was about to answer, and I was listening as if his words held a life-or-death secret, when the tram stopped.

'Here we are at the Palacio de los Consejos already,' said Rafael. 'We'd better get off.'

Oh no! They were leaving before I could find out how the story ended.

'Sir, sir, a word!' I said when I saw them getting up.

The young man paused and looked at me.

'What about the Countess? What happened to the Countess?' I asked eagerly.

The only response I received was the laughter of the other passengers. The two young men, who were also laughing, left without a word. The only human creature who retained her sphinx-like serenity during this comical scene was the Englishwoman, who, indignant at my eccentric behaviour, turned to the other passengers and said:

'The man's a lunatic!'

XII

The tram set off again, and I was burning with curiosity to know what had become of the poor Countess. Did her husband kill her? I knew what the wretch's intentions were. Like all cruel souls, he was eager to have his revenge and wanted his wife to stand by helplessly and watch the death agony of that unwary youth, drawn there by the vile trap set by Mudarra.

But how could the lady continue desperately to maintain her calm, when she knew Rafael had drunk the poison? A truly tragic, blood-curdling scene, I thought, more and more convinced of the reality of the event. And people say these things only happen in novels!

As we passed the Palace, the tram stopped again, and a woman carrying a little dog got on. I immediately recognized the dog I had seen curled at the Countess's feet; it was the same animal, with the same fine white hair and the same black spot on one of its ears. Fate decreed that this woman should then sit down next to me. Unable to contain my curiosity, I asked her:

'Is that pretty little dog yours?'

'Of course. Do you like him?'

I made to stroke one of the intelligent creature's ears, but the dog, misinterpreting this display of affection, barked and jumped onto the Englishwoman's lap, who again showed me her sharp teeth, as if she were about to bite me, exclaiming:

'You are *incorrigible!*'

'And where did you get the dog?' I asked, ignoring the Englishwoman's latest choleric outburst. 'If you don't mind my asking, that is.'

'It belonged to my mistress.'

'And what happened to your mistress?' I asked urgently.

'Oh, did you know her?' replied the woman. 'She was so very kind, wasn't she?'

'Oh, yes, a fine woman. But what exactly happened?'

'So you know about it? You've heard the news?'

'Indeed. I know precisely what happened up until that business with the tea ... So the lady died, did she?'

'Yes, God rest her.'

'But how? Was she murdered or was it as a consequence of the shock?'

'What do you mean "murdered"? What "shock"?' she said, a mocking look on her face. 'You haven't heard the news, have you? She ate something that night which disagreed with her. She had a funny turn and had to take to her bed, where she remained until morning.'

'Huh!' I thought. 'She either knows nothing about the incident with the piano and the poison or else is pretending that she doesn't.'

Then I said:

'So it was something she ate, was it?'

'Yes. I said to her that night: "Don't eat the seafood, Señora," but she took no notice.'

'Seafood?' I said incredulously. 'Don't give me that.'

'Don't you believe me?'

'Yes, yes, of course,' I said, pretending that I did. 'And what about the Count?'

'What Count?'

'Her husband, the Countess's husband, the one who took out his dagger while she was playing the piano.'

The woman looked at me for a moment, then laughed in my face.

'You may laugh, but don't think I don't know what really happened. You obviously don't want to give me the true version of events. Well, we'll see about that. This is a criminal case!'

'But you mentioned a Count and a Countess.'

'Wasn't the Countess the owner of the dog and her butler a man called Mudarra?'

The woman again roared with laughter, so loudly this time that I said to myself: 'She must be Mudarra's accomplice and is clearly trying to conceal the truth.'

'You're mad,' she said.

'Oh, yes, the man's a complete lunatic. He nearly suffocated me!' cried the Englishwoman.

'I know everything. Don't try to hide the truth from me. Tell me how the Countess really died.'

'What Countess are you talking about, man?' asked the woman, bursting out laughing again.

'Look, don't think you can fool me with your guffawing,' I replied. 'The Countess was either poisoned or murdered; I'm absolutely sure of it.'

XIII

The tram reached the *barrio* of Pozas, and I the end of my journey. We all got off. The Englishwoman shot me a glance indicating her delight at being free of me at last, and everyone went their separate ways. I followed the woman with the dog, bombarding her with questions, until she reached her house and went in, still laughing at my insistence on poking my nose into other people's lives. Finding myself alone in the street, I remembered the original object of my journey and made my way to the house where I was to deliver the books. I returned them to the person who had lent them to me and then strolled up and down near the church of Buen Suceso, waiting for the tram to return and take me back to the other side of Madrid.

I couldn't stop thinking about the unfortunate Countess and was becoming more and more convinced that the woman I had spoken to on the tram had wanted to deceive me by hiding the truth about the whole mysterious tragedy.

XIV

It was getting dark when the tram was ready to depart. I climbed on board, and who do you think I saw? The Englishwoman, sitting in the very same seat. When she spotted me and when I again sat down beside her, the expression on her face was indescribable. She once more turned bright scarlet and exclaimed:

'Not you again! I'll have to complain to the conductor.'

So immersed was I in my tangled thoughts that, ignoring what the Englishwoman was saying to me in her laborious, hybrid Spanish, I said:

'There is no doubt in my mind that the Countess was either poisoned or murdered. You have no idea how ruthless that man is.'

The tram moved off, stopping every now and then to pick up passengers. Near the Palacio Real, three people got on and sat down opposite me. One of them was a tall, thin, bony man with very hard eyes and a resonant voice that commanded respect.

They had not been seated ten minutes when the man turned to his companions and said:

'The poor thing! How she cried out in her last moments. The bullet entered above her right clavicle and then penetrated her heart.'

'What?' I exclaimed, addressing myself to them. 'You mean she was shot? Wasn't she stabbed to death?'

The three men stared at me in surprise.

'No, she was shot,' declared the tall, thin, bony man in a rather surly tone of voice.

'And yet that woman claimed she'd died of food poisoning,' I said, feeling more intrigued by the minute. 'Tell me, what happened?'

'What has it got to do with you?' asked the man sourly.

'I'm very keen to know how this terrible tragedy ended. It's like something out of a novel, isn't it?'

'What do you mean "a novel"? You're either mad or you're making fun of us.'

'This is no joking matter, sir,' said the tall, thin man.

'Do you think I don't know? I know everything. I was a witness to various scenes from this horrible crime. But you say the Countess died from a bullet wound.'

'For heaven's sake, we weren't talking about a Countess, but about my dog who got shot accidentally while we were out hunting. If you want to joke, then we can meet elsewhere and I'll give you the answer you deserve.'

'I see. Now you want to cover up the truth,' I said, believing that they wanted to put me off the track by making the poor Countess into a dog.

The man was just preparing his riposte, doubtless a more violent one than the situation called for, when the Englishwoman tapped her forehead as if to tell them that I wasn't quite right in the head. They calmed down then and didn't say another word for the rest of the journey, which ended for them in Puerta del Sol. They were probably afraid of me.

XV

I was still totally consumed by this business and quite incapable of quietening my mind, however hard I tried to reason my way through the whole complex matter. Instead, I grew even more confused and was quite unable to get the image of the poor woman out of my head. I seemed to see in every one of the ever-changing faces on the tram some fact that might contribute to explaining the enigma. My brain was horribly over-excited and that inner turmoil must have shown on my face, because everyone was staring at me as one might stare at some extraordinary sight.

XVI

Another thing occurred to trouble my poor head on that ill-fated journey. As we were travelling along Calle de

Alcalá, a man and a woman got on, and the man sat down next to me. He seemed deeply affected by some recent shocking event, and I even thought I saw him raise his handkerchief to his eyes now and then to dry the invisible tears he was doubtless shedding behind the green lenses of his huge spectacles.

After a while, the man said softly to the woman who appeared to be his wife:

'There are suspicions that she may have been poisoned, you know. Don Mateo just told me. The poor woman!'

'How dreadful! I'd wondered about that myself,' replied his consort. 'But what can you expect from such villains?'

'I swear I'll leave no stone unturned to find out.'

Then I, all ears, said in an equally low voice:

'It's true, sir, there was a poisoning. I know that for a fact.'

'What? You know? You knew her too?' said the man in the green spectacles eagerly, turning to me.

'Yes, she suffered a violent death, of that I am quite sure, however much certain people would like us to believe it was food poisoning.'

'My feelings exactly. She was such an excellent woman too. But how do you know?'

'I just know,' I said, pleased that he didn't take me for a madman.

'Then you must testify in court. They're drawing up the indictment now.'

'I'd be glad to and to see those scoundrels punished. Oh, I'll testify all right.'

My obsession had reached such extremes that I had allowed that event, half-dreamed, half-read-about, to take me over entirely, and I believed it as surely as I believe this is a pen with which I'm writing.

'Indeed, sir, we must clear up this enigma so that the perpetrators of the crime can be punished. I will testify that she was poisoned with a cup of tea, just like the young man.'

'Did you hear that, Petronila?' said the man in the spectacles to his wife. 'A cup of tea!'

'I'm astonished,' answered the lady. 'The lengths these men will go to.'

'Yes, a cup of tea. The Countess was playing the piano...'

'What Countess?' asked the man, interrupting me.

'The Countess, the one who was poisoned.'

'We're not talking about a Countess, man!'

'So you're another one determined to cover the whole thing up.'

'No, no. There was no Countess or Duchess involved, but the laundress who lives in the same building as us, the pointsman's wife.'

'A laundress, eh?' I said mischievously. 'So you want me to believe that she was a laundress, do you?'

The man and his wife looked at me mockingly, then mumbled something to each other. From a gesture the woman made, I realized that they were convinced I was drunk. I stoically said nothing more, opting to treat that disrespectful supposition with the silent scorn proper to large souls. My anxiety was growing. The Countess did not leave my thoughts for a second, and I had become as deeply concerned about her sinister end as if the whole affair were not the result of the unhealthy lucubrations of my own imagination, under the influence of successive chance encounters and conversations. In order that you can see to what extremes my madness brought me, I will describe the final incident on that journey and the extravagant way in which I brought to a close that painful struggle with my reason, embroiled as it was in that battle of shadows.

XVII

The tram was just entering Calle de Serrano, when I looked out through the window ahead of me at the dimly lit street. I saw a man walking past and I cried out in surprise and shouted wildly:

'There he is, there is cruel Mudarra himself, the perpetrator of all those crimes!'

I told the tram to stop and scrambled to the door, stumbling over the feet and legs of the other passengers. Once in the street, I ran after the man, yelling:

'Stop that man! He's a murderer!'

You can imagine the effect of these cries in that peaceful area of Madrid.

Passers-by detained the man—the very man I had seen earlier in the tram—while I bawled:

'He's the one who prepared the poison for the Countess, the one who killed the Countess!'

There was a moment of indescribable confusion. He said I was mad, and, of course, we were both immediately marched off to the police station. I have no recollection of what happened after that. I cannot remember what I did that night in the place where they locked me up. My most vivid recollection after these strange events is of waking from the deep lethargy into which I fell, a drunkenness of the mind produced by what exactly I really don't know, by one of those passing episodes of mental derangement of such interest to scientists as the precursors of hopeless insanity.

As you can imagine, nothing came of the matter, for the unpleasant fellow I had named Mudarra was, in fact, an honest grocer who had never poisoned a single Countess in his life. And yet, for a long time afterwards, I persisted in my delusion and would cry out:

'Poor unfortunate Countess! Whatever the others may say, I still stick to my guns. No one will persuade me that you did not end your days at the hands of your enraged husband.'

XVIII

It has taken some months for these ghosts to return to the mysterious place whence they arose to drive me to the brink of insanity, and for reality to re-establish itself in my mind again. I laugh now when I think of that tram ride, and the concern I once felt for that imagined victim and which I now devote—would you believe it?—to my companion on that distressing journey, the irascible English-woman, whose foot I dislocated when I was rushing to get off the tram in pursuit of the supposed butler.

Madrid, November 1871

The Solution

Emilia Pardo Bazán

You could set your watch by her: at three o'clock each afternoon in winter, and at five o'clock in summer, Frasquita Llerena would set off for the Retiro Park accompanied by her griffon Mosquito, tiny as a toy and tethered by a strong red silk cord, one end of which was tied to the ring of the pretty little white leather collar complete with silver bells. The little creature was a perfect picture: his silky grey hair formed a curtain over his small, shiny, black snout, and behind that silken blind, his huge eyes were like two ripe grapes, sweet and ready to eat. When Mosquito grew tired, Frasquita would pick him up in her arms. And the only reason she regretted having no carriage of her own was that she had no cosy cushioned corner in which to ensconce Mosquito.

She was an old maid, but quite happy with her freedom, and her dog was the one thing she cared about. She washed him, deloused him, and perfumed him with real eau de cologne; she herself served him his astonishing diet of custard and rice balls; she even cleaned his teeth with tooth powder and brush. On December nights, she would jump out of bed, barefoot, to make sure the little dog was safely asleep on his feather pillow beneath a microscopic blanket made of quilted satin. During the day, she would take him out for a 'breath of fresh air'. Entrust him to the maid? Why, she would be sure to lose him or let someone else steal him!

One splendid Sunday afternoon in April, walking along the packed pavements of Calle de Alcalá, Frasquita had a strange feeling, as if she had suddenly been left alone in the crowd. Before she could realize what had happened, she bumped into a mature gentleman of her acquaintance, Don Santos Comares de la Puente, a senior official at the Treasury. He smiled and greeted her and, in accordance with Spanish custom, stopped for a moment to ask after her health. When the good gentleman vanished into the crowd waiting for the pre-bullfight parade, Frasquita again felt strangely alone. The red silk lead hung loose, cut; Mosquito had disappeared.

Frasquita had the reserved, energetic nature typical of many women who reach the age of forty without the shelter and warmth of a family. She did not shout or make a fuss. She looked around her. There was no sign of the dog nor of anyone who looked as if they might have taken him. She asked the concierges in the houses nearby; she informed the police and even offered a reward; she put advertisements in the newspapers; she paid for a mass to St Anthony, the patron saint of things lost. Mosquito wasn't lost though, he had been stolen, which is why St Anthony could not help. Thieves were not his responsibility.

After two months, with still no sign of the griffon, Frasquita fell ill with jaundice. To dispel her sadness, she was advised to walk a lot, along streets, in cheerful crowded places. As she stood before a shop window in Carrera de San Jerónimo, she suddenly saw reflected in the clear glass a shape as familiar as it was adored: her little love! She turned, repressing a cry of wild joy and, just as she had when the dog first disappeared, she found herself before the somewhat inelegant figure of Don Santos Comares, who, again, greeted her and enquired cordially, but somewhat tiresomely after her health. This time, however, beneath the cuff of the functionary's left sleeve, between his arm and his body, she saw Mosquito's adorable little head peeking out, his eyes like ripe grapes, and heard him give his comical, falsetto bark, overjoyed to see his former mistress.

'My boy! My treasure! Light of my life! Sweetheart!'

When she leaned forward to seize the dog, Don Santos, on the defensive, retreated in order to protect the 'prey' with a shocked and indignant cry of 'Señora!' that made passers-by exchange ironical, smiling looks.

'I love him! He's mine, and now I know who took him from me. It was you, that same afternoon, in Calle de Alcalá,' Frasquita declared, beside herself with rage, ready to come to blows.

'Señora!' repeated Don Santos, retreating still further and ready to defend the dog with his life. 'Do you take me for a dog-thief? This little creature belongs to me, I bought him (and he wasn't cheap either), with my own money. I've even registered him, and I will not have anyone disputing my ownership.'

'But you must have seen my initials and his name on the collar. See how he responds to me, how he looks at me. Mosquito! Don't you know me, sweetie?'

'When I acquired him, Señora, he had no collar. I ordered a new one from Melerio, and renamed the dog Togo. I'm a great admirer of the Japanese admiral of that name, you see. Eh, Togo? See him wagging his tail!'

Frasquita, in despair, felt her eyes filling with tears. A crowd was beginning to gather and some were making coarse remarks. Decorum won out over passion. Shaking, she said in a low, hoarse voice:

'Fine, Señor Comares, fine. Take what is not yours. When you feel sufficiently ashamed of what you have done, I hope you will restore him to me. I thought you were a gentleman. Off you go, if you still have the heart to enjoy what was torn so rudely from me. That's why Spain is in the state it is, because we tolerate such pranks!'

And without shaking her rival's hand, she turned her back on him and set off towards Calle de Sevilla, followed by a hundred curious, malevolently jeering eyes.

Her health deteriorated. The doctor who attended her knew what was destroying that body and torturing that mind, and when he visited Señor Comares, who was another of his patients, to prescribe some mineral water, he told him the situation. Señor Comares was not a heartless fellow. He asked Frasquita if he could visit and took Mosquito with him and placed him on the spinster's lap.

'I am most upset, Señora, really most upset. I cannot give you back the dog, but I will bring him to see you whenever I have a few minutes, so that you can stroke him and see how plump and healthy he is.'

'Are you mocking me?' she cried angrily. 'Under those conditions, I would rather not even see my dear little dog. What, bring him and then take him away again? How could you even think such a thing? What an idea!'

'Calm down, Frasquita. We are all human and we all have our affections and our feelings. Ever since I lost my only boy, in whom I had placed so many hopes, and, as a result, lost my wife as well, and after a series of griefs, which, if I recounted them, would move you to tears ... well, there's no one to keep me company, and I've grown fond of the little chap. He's such a sweet creature. You can insult me all you wish, but I won't give Togo back to you, and that's that. That's how I feel.'

Frasquita said nothing, but sat there, frowning and thoughtful. Suddenly, she leapt up from the chaise longue, grabbed the dog, flung open the window, and, dangling the griffon out in space, exclaimed tragically:

'If you try to steal him from me again, I'll drop him.'

Don Santos froze. He could already imagine his Togo lying shattered on the pavement below, his large eyes closed, his little head smashed on the paving stones, his silken hair lying limp, his little feet cold ... The woman had triumphed. The fury of love had won out over calm, nostalgic affection.

The following morning, Frasquita received a polite note from Don Santos, asking permission to visit the house. That way, he could see Togo now and then and bring *her* some chocolates.

How could she refuse? The victor kindly welcomed her defeated opponent. So different were they in character that they got on famously; they grew accustomed to seeing each other and to putting up with each other's foibles, the foibles of two ageing, solitary souls ... After a year, the dog belonged to them both equally and rode in the carriage with his master and mistress. However, the husband always called him Togo and the wife Mosquito.

Sunday Morning

Alonso Zamora Vicente

My father took me everywhere. He is bound up in my memory with all the small pleasures of my childhood. Sometimes it was the dog cart in Plaza de Oriente, which had three classes of traveller: the rider on the mule, the coachman in his seat, and the passengers. The cart, hung with little bells that we would jangle wildly, trotted us round the oval-shaped garden flanked by large acacias and surrounded by statues of kings (they all look the same, Papa) while we gnawed at the wafer the woman always gave us when we climbed aboard. At other times— every Sunday morning—it was the changing of the guard at the Palacio Real. I would climb the railings and from there, with my face pressed between two of the iron bars, I would watch the strange ceremony, the to and fro of the horses, the raised swords (what are they saying to each other, do they never fight?), cannons being hauled about, while the two bands took it in turn to play paso dobles. Some days, my father would say: 'Look at the King on the balcony over there,' and I could never see anyone on that vast façade, or if I did, he looked nothing like the photos in the newspapers. Then we would walk slowly back, identifying the different regiments by their uniforms—the Princess's hussars, the hussars of Pavia, the lancers of Alcalá, the Royal Escort—and my father would hold my hand tightly or else pick me up so that I could watch them pass by.

We always stopped midway across the Viaduct, where we would shudder to think of those who had thrown themselves off, the poor suicides (don't worry, they always throw themselves off at night, when no one else is around). It was the old iron viaduct, which had the look of a dirty, rusty tin can, with its high handrail, the blind man clutching a notice, which said something about 'gutta serena', and a dog holding a saucer in its mouth to receive any donations. It was while looking out from the Viaduct that I learned the names of the tall churches, the winding streets and secret corners of which I grew so fond. The Convento de las Bernardas looming over the Palacio de los Consejos, its broad-shouldered tower always leaning slightly backwards so as not to fall into the ravine

of Calle de Segovia; the spires of San Miguel, the Town Hall, and Santa Cruz, like childish adornments, castles made of dominos; the cathedral with its two low, blunt towers in front of its cupola; a vague memory of a seated lion with its claws out. San Pedro, with its owl-faced brick tower, and San Andrés, very tall and slender, looking proud to have reached the top of its steep narrow street. And then there were the open spaces, Casa de Campo further off and Paseo de la Florida, the smoke from the trains and the names of the distant mountains: Montón de Trigo, La Maliciosa, Peñalara, Siete Picos, Abantos.*
'There's the Escorial,' my father would say, pointing. And I could never see that either, only houses, hills, the occasional cloud, and endless horizons, none of which resembled the Escorial, that building of many towers and lots of dark slate that I'd seen in books or on a penholder made out of bone with a little glass hole in it, a souvenir someone had brought me, although I can't remember how or when. On the other hand, I do know that if you closed one eye and looked through the hole, you could see six pictures, three at a time, including one of a very dead king, Charles V apparently, and which I deliberately avoided because I didn't want to have nightmares.

* Pile of wheat, Mischief-maker, [Peñalara—no specific meaning], Seven Peaks, Vultures.

Late morning, with the midday sun filling the little Plaza de San Andrés, and my father strolling up and down with Don Juan the parish priest. I never knew what they talked about so seriously, utterly oblivious to everything else. At first, I would follow them, until boredom got the better of me. Then I would go and sit on a bench beside the church and watch them, my father nodding or shrugging, his hands behind his back, the light always catching the same folds on Don Juan's cassock, both men in perfect step. Now and then, in the atrium, gusts of wind would whip up swirls of dust that I would chase and try to stamp on. My father and Don Juan came and went. I didn't dare interrupt them. I could escape with the other boys and they wouldn't notice. And then when we got home, Elisa would bawl, where have you been, look at the state of your boots, anyone would think you were a street urchin, while my father would wonder how I could possibly have got my boots in that state and assure Elisa wearily that we had only been to see the parade, and I would cry, yes, we've been to the parade and seen the King ever so close *and* the Escorial, and later, when no one could hear me, in case what I wanted to know was really obvious or perhaps rude, I would ask my father the meaning of those words 'gutta serena' on the blind man's notice.

Yes, perhaps my clearest recollection from that time are those Sunday mornings. My anxiety on Saturday, when it still wasn't certain that we would go, or only if the weather was fine or if there was nothing else to do. Not after the way you behaved, you'll run off again, you tore your trousers. I slept lightly in anticipation and tried to guess from the morning glow outside the window what kind of day it would be. From my bed, I learned to tell how cold it was, or whether or not we would go and watch the parade, by deciphering the various noises from the street, the repeated cries of streetsellers, the quality of the light or the gleam on a piece of furniture or a tile. Then, without even having to ask, my father and I would exchange a look, and the decision was made. Off we went down Calle de Don Pedro (mind the puddles), we could already hear the soldiers and then we saw the uniforms and the mountains and that bend in the river, give me your hand to cross the road, look, there's a space, and once more I would climb the railings, see those raised swords, hear the bells rung at eleven o'clock, and on the way back, are we going to visit Don Juan, and can I have one of those, the King didn't appear today, he must be working, and don't run your hand along the wall like that, and I return now, with no landscape, no colours, just a distant wind, and I am absorbed by life into an accumulation of silence, slow and complete.

A Testing Time

Juan García Hortelano

A long time ago, when I was a child, it snowed a lot. I remember.

Ángel González

In early December, the first snow fell. A week later, it snowed for three whole days and nights. The trenches filled up to the top and the barricades grew an extra two feet. The strange light of those afternoons—and the odd excitement of the mornings—would find us, as it grew dark, standing very still and silent in doorways. The nearby fields, the empty plots and pavements, which had been muddy until then, were now grey or white, depending on the time of day and on how much new snow had fallen. In our houses, after supper, we would listen intently, almost anxiously to the radio.

The morning when Tano got his head split open was the first of that period of constant snow. When we went outside, it felt like dusk, although, in fact, it was only midday. On the top of the last barricade, which was shaped like a kind of curved pyramid, someone had placed a red flag. We paraded up and down in front of the flag several times, singing songs from the front, our feet deep in snow. Then we started throwing snowballs. Someone—unintentionally, because we were all part of the same gang—must have picked up a stone by mistake when making his snowball. The blow struck Tano on the right temple, and Tano sat down as if he'd been punched in the stomach, then, very slowly, leaned back until he was lying down. As we picked him up by his arms and legs, the wound began to bleed.

By the time we reached the first landing, the concierge was screaming and when, to my dismay, Luisa found me outside Tano's apartment, she dragged me upstairs. Over lunch, my grandfather, who had gone down straight away to tend to Tano, said that one day we'd end up killing each other, because we were clearly completely out of control. My father, Luisa, and he got very steamed up and said over and over that there was to be no more playing in the street with those louts; only my grandmother continued to eat in silence and, whenever our eyes met, she would smile at me. Luisa sent me off to take my afternoon nap, half-closed the shutters, and told me that, when the war was over, Mama would want nothing to do with me. It was cosy under the blankets and I lay there thinking about Concha.

The brightness from the snow outside meant that I could glimpse a few low, black clouds through the window. It seemed to be dark already. After Riánsares had given me my bread and hot chocolate, I went into the living room, kissed Grandma, and then went out into the street. It must have been about half past six. On the corner of the Paseo, some boys were building a snowman alongside the big snowball we'd made earlier that morning. I went over to help, but I felt worried, most of all about Tano, who would still be in bed. When we'd had enough of the intense cold burning our hands despite our woollen gloves, we talked a bit about the coming demonstration. I decided to go and wait for Concha, but when I found myself alone by the wall of the old convent, I again thought of Tano.

As soon as I sat down in the wicker chair beside his bed, I could tell he was in a bad mood.

'Are you fed up?'

He didn't even look at me. Propped up against various bolsters and pillows, he continued sipping his malt drink, then gave me a biscuit and told me to take down from the shelf the novels of Jules Verne, Salgari, and the 'Brave Men' series.

'What, all of them?'

'Yes, all of them.'

Then he called his mother so that she could remove the tray and we could spread the books out on his bed, but once we'd done that, he didn't even touch them. He pressed one hand to his bandage, which made him look rather like a Moor, and closed his eyes.

'Does it hurt?' I asked. The Jules Verne books were mine. 'Grandpa says we'll end up killing each other one of these days.' After Christmas I'd ask for them back whether he'd read them or not. 'It's seven o'clock, you know. Concha will have gone to fetch the milk. She's probably already heard about you getting hit on the head.' Perhaps it was really painful. 'I'll leave if you like.' He opened his eyes for a moment. 'Apparently, there's going to be a demonstration tomorrow.'

'So they haven't taken down the flag yet?'

'No,' I said.

Then he started asking about the others in the gang, as if he'd been in bed for years. He was wearing a really nice pair of blue pyjamas that I'd never seen before. He ordered me to put the books back on the shelf, but it didn't occur to me that he was hinting I should leave, because I was still telling him about the demonstration. He again called his mother and this time asked for an aspirin. She told me I should go because Tano needed to sleep, and that my grandfather and my father were in the living room with Tano's father, playing cards. I said I was going home, and Tano perhaps knew I was lying.

The kerb lay hidden beneath the snow, and I stood leaning against the gate of Señor Pedro's coalyard. It was very cold, and standing there in the slowly falling snow was a bit like being Michael Strogoff, except that you couldn't be Michael Strogoff for very long without freezing and, besides, I was thinking less about that Courier of the Tsar's dangerous missions than I was about Concha and Tano.

Over supper, no one asked if I'd done my French homework or said anything about how we boys would end up killing one another, no one mentioned God's hand or how upset Mama (on the Other Side) would be. And when they all sat down around the radio, like the branches of a tree, I went off to bed without being told to. I started thinking how sad I had felt standing next to the metal gate of the coalyard, then I thought of Concha's body. Grandma came to tuck me in, but, by then, I was already almost asleep.

From the open ground at the end of the Paseo, we heard the sound of marching feet. There were more red flags on the barricades, and placards swayed back and forth above the crowd advancing down the street. We started running. I enjoyed singing 'To the barricades'* because

* Popular song among anarchists during the Civil War.

I knew all the words, and I liked 'If you want to write to me' too, because there were lots of different versions. We marched down unfamiliar streets. For a while, I helped hold up one of the placards; later, I fell behind and grew hoarse with shouting: '¡No pasarán!'—'They will not pass!'—and 'They will not pass, they will not pass, but if they do, they die!', which was more rousing somehow and helped us keep in step as we marched through the snow and the mud. I thought occasionally of Concha, but didn't see her face in the crowd. It was snowing hard, almost furiously, and the wind pricked our faces with needles of cold. Our gang had got split up, and so I returned home alone and late, and was punished by having to eat my meal in the kitchen.

Riánsares was eating standing up, always ready to respond to the demands of Luisa, the stove, her own plate of food, and the sink. I let my family believe that being relegated to the kitchen was a punishment, but actually I preferred it there, sitting opposite the courtyard window that looked out over the garden of the former convent, watching Riánsares coming and going, and seeing the backs of her knees when she bent over the sink. Besides, if you knew how, it was always possible to wheedle some news about Concha out of her.

'How was the demonstration?'

'Oh, great,' I said.

'I bet it was. I tried to see what was going on from the balcony, but it was snowing.'

'We sang and we shouted. And sometimes we just walked along in silence, as if we were singing to ourselves. It was really great.'

'Eat your bread. There's plenty left over.'

'There were flags and placards too, saying that Madrid will be the graveyard of fascism.'

'I'm glad to hear it. Now eat that bread up. Were there any nurses there?'

'Nurses? No, there were a lot of militiawomen. Some even had rifles. They say that if the men haven't got the balls for it ...'

'Don't let your sister hear you saying "balls"!'

'Why don't you sit down?'

'I like eating standing up.'

'Anyway, they were saying that if the men aren't up to it, they'll go to the front in their place. I didn't see any nurses, though. You know, Tano says Concha's only fifteen.'

'Fifteen! She's at least eighteen or nineteen. I'm seventeen, and she's older than me.'

'Older than you?' I caught a glimpse of Riánsares's reddened, almost round thighs. 'Tano says she isn't.'

'Honestly, you two, that's all you think about. Have you eaten all your bread?' When she heard Luisa ring the bell,

Riánsares immediately put the pudding plates on a tray. 'Concha's no spring chicken and she's a right tart too.'

Whenever Riánsares called other women 'tarts', I flushed scarlet, as if I were touching their two bodies. After drinking my malt drink made with condensed milk, I crept quietly over to the sink and put my hands up Riánsares's skirt. She seemed so startled that I thought perhaps she was genuinely angry. And there we stayed until Luisa came to find me and send me off for my nap.

Afterwards, I went and stood for a while by the convent wall and, later, I perched on the ledge at one corner, but as soon as it struck seven, I went up to see Tano. He was wearing different pyjamas and his bandage had been changed too. I told him about the fate of fascism, about the militiawomen, the placards, and singing '¡No pasarán!', but Tano, who never listened to what you were saying, wanted to tell me the story of *The Red Corsair*. He gave me two biscuits from his teatime snack.

'They made me have my lunch in the kitchen today. Riánsares says Concha's older than you think.' Tano gestured to me to shut the bedroom door before getting out his packet of herbal cigarettes. 'What do you reckon?'

'It's possible,' said Tano.

'She says Concha's a tart.'

Tano was seized by a fit of coughing after the first puff, and I was afraid he might change the subject once he was able to speak again.

'Riánsares is just jealous,' he said at last.

'Why?'

'Because Concha's a lady and she's a maid, a peasant.'

'But,' I insisted, 'Concha probably *is* a bit of a tart, don't you think?'

'Like I said, she's a lady.'

'Sometimes, though, she lets us touch her up.'

He smiled, as if he knew perfectly well—as did I—how very little Concha let us do.

'That's because we're gentlemen.'

'Us?'

'Yes, us. Anyway, I'm not interested in what your maid has to say.'

'If we're gentlemen,' I said, and at this point, Tano opened the book, 'why do we carry a catapult and blaspheme and touch women's bottoms?' The look in his eyes made me blush, reminding me, as it did, that he was the Leader. 'Why? Tell me that!'

'Don't shout! Mama might come in,' he said, handing me what remained of the cigarette, so that I could throw it out into the street. 'Because now we're at war.'

'So what?'

'Well, after the war, we won't touch women's bottoms and we won't blaspheme. And we'll all have to go to school.'

'I'm going to keep blaspheming until I die.'

'No you won't, because the Nationalists are going to win.'

'They're not. That's not what they were saying at the demonstration this morning.' The unseemly creaking of the wicker chair beneath me fired my anger. 'According to them, Madrid will be the graveyard of fascism.'

'Fine, but you ask your father or mine what they hear on the radio. Go on, ask them.' That was when Tano gave me the second biscuit. 'Your grandfather said that, if I'm good, I can get out of bed the day after tomorrow.'

'I don't care what they hear on their poxy radio, you can hardly hear it anyway.' The cigarette was burning my fingers and I got up to open the balcony window. 'You said once that all grown-ups are liars.' Tano turned his face to the wall and complained of a headache. 'Anyway, if you are allowed up the day after tomorrow, we can go and wait for her.'

'Who?'

'Concha.'

But then he started telling me the story of *The Red Corsair* and *The Green Corsair*, because he never took any notice of what you said to him. I was feeling tired and a bit sad and didn't want to remind him yet again that I'd read them already, nor that I wasn't bothered about school, because I was having classes with Doña Berthe. And so I let him talk until he had cheered himself up, which almost cheered me up too.

In bed, listening to my sister Luisa telling my grandmother that it was still snowing, I decided to pretend to be asleep if they came in to say the rosary. I swore that the following day, whatever happened, I would find Concha. I woke in the morning calculating how many hours it was until seven o'clock.

That night's snowfall, even heavier than on the previous days, had covered the muddy ice on the barricades and the pavements. The light in the silent street hurt my eyes. When I said I was going with Riánsares to join the queue outside the baker's, I was told to be sure to wear my wellington boots.

The women in the queue were talking nineteen to the dozen, breaking into unexpected quarrels and waving their arms about. One of them said that the war was going well and that we were giving them a good thrashing. Leaning on a tree, with the snow almost up to my knees, I glanced over to see which of them had said this and that was when I saw Concha at the back of the queue. As usual, I was aware of her full lips and her rather throaty, almost mannish laugh. I went up to her and she placed her hand on the back of my neck.

'Did you hear about Tano getting hit on the head?'

She didn't hear me and I had to repeat the question, and, even though we were the same height, she bent her head slightly and put her arm around my shoulders.

'You'll kill each other one of these days.'

'It was an accident, a joke. It was only us local lads. By the way, are you going to fetch the milk this evening?'

Riánsares came to join us, putting away her ration coupons in her bread bag. She and Concha made me nervous with all their chatter, and so I went over to the coalyard to see Señor Pedro, who was wearing a beret to cover his bald head. It was colder than ever that morning. We talked about the snow, about Tano, about the soapbox car with ball-bearing wheels that I'd been making for the last six months, modelled on one Señor Pedro had built. Then he was summoned indoors by his wife and I was left out in the street, not quite knowing what to do or who to talk to. I saw this person and that, but we all seemed rather lethargic somehow, but at the same time filled with a feeling that, in some way we couldn't quite put our finger on, we should have been making the most of the snow. I went back to the baker's, but Concha had gone. In the end, I went up to see Tano.

He was in such a good mood that the time passed quickly. He didn't even get annoyed when I told him that I wouldn't be getting my pocket money until Sunday and that I didn't have a single cigarette to my name. On the contrary, he gave me one of his, and we puffed away together. He didn't make me take all the books down from the bookshelf either, and we planned a lot of things for the following day, and so engrossed were we in talking that Luisa had to come downstairs to fetch me for lunch. Grandpa announced that, from now on, we would say the rosary after our afternoon nap, so that then we could listen to the radio in peace at night. I remembered that I'd forgotten to tell Tano that the war was going well, and that we were giving the other side a real thrashing. I woke up early from my nap, kissed my grandmother, and went out into the street. It was still dark.

Sitting on the ledge, I was assailed by complicated thoughts as I waited and waited, with no idea what time it was and feeling tempted sometimes to just give up and leave. When Tano was there, we never had to wait that long. We would be playing together and then, suddenly, there she would be, walking towards us. Not that me and Tano waited for her every day, and there wasn't usually all that snow around or that piercing cold. So as not to freeze, I ran up and down the black street. Later, I took shelter in the gateway of the old coachyard in the Paseo. There was something frightening about the Paseo that evening, and it was then that it occurred to me that perhaps Tano thought *I* had thrown the stone. I couldn't remember anything about it, just as if I'd never even taken part in the snowball fight, but I made a decision to confess to Tano that I had touched Concha. It was sad to think that the snow would melt and that those strange days would come to an end, along with the oddly exciting fear provoked by the snowy darkness, the solitude and the cold, and Tano being confined to bed.

When I caught sight of her green overcoat and woollen hat, I didn't immediately jump down from my perch on the windowsill.

'What are you doing here in the dark?'

'Shall I carry your milk can?'

'No, let's go home. Mind you don't slip.'

'You be careful too.' A few locks of fair hair had escaped from beneath her hat. 'You're looking very pretty.'

She laughed, as if to herself, while we walked slowly along. She kept close to the red brick wall and I kept blowing on my bare hands to warm them.

'D'you know what,' I said, unconsciously imitating the way Tano sometimes spoke, 'I was waiting for you.'

'I know,' said Concha.

In the doorway, she put the can down on the ground, and my hands flew generously and swiftly to her hips and breasts. Unusually, she pushed me away, with a brusqueness I didn't at first understand, and when we emerged once more into the darkness of the street, she seemed anxious to get away. By the convent wall, though, she stood still for what seemed an eternity and I thought my trembling hands would freeze. When I kissed her for the first time, she giggled slightly. Then she let me embrace her, in silence and without pushing me away, and, at one point, I realized that she was returning my embrace and into my mind came the little I knew—from muddled conversations with Tano and the other boys—about men and women.

'OK, that's enough,' she said suddenly.

'Are you angry?'

'Don't talk when you kiss, all right?'

'But I didn't say anything,' I said, withdrawing my hands.

'It's getting late. Goodbye.'

'Bye.'

She turned round in the doorway, and I ran to her.

'Don't tell anyone, OK? Real men don't tell. Not your sister Luisa, not Tano, not ...'

'Do you want me to bring Luisa with me when I come to see you at home?'

'No.'

'Are you my girlfriend now?'

'Look, it's really late. I'll see you tomorrow.'

The following day, Tano still didn't get out of bed, and Concha and I spent only a short time together. I had supper in the kitchen, because I was now permanently in disgrace. Even Riánsares told me off when she came back from serving pudding.

'Your grandfather and father are furious with you because you're always off out somewhere. You're turning into a right little lout, or are you one already?'

'Here you are,' I gave her half of the orange I had just peeled. 'No, I'm not a lout. I study hard and I do my homework. By the time the holidays are over, I'll have done all the homework I was set. Tell me something, Riánsares, are you not supposed to talk to a girl while you're feeling her up?'

'You see, you *are* a lout. With girls,' she said, 'you'd be better off not touching them at all.'

'Why not? It's nice and they like it.'

'If your father and grandfather find out ...'

'We're going to win the war, Riánsares.'

'I'm not so sure. Some say one thing and others another. Think of those poor men stuck in a trench on a night like this. Go on, off you go to the fire.'

'I haven't finished my supper yet. So are you supposed to talk to them or not?'

'What do you think?'

'I think you can, but only a little bit. Is that right?'

'Well, you're not going to touch me.'

'I wasn't going to.'

'Good, just so that's clear...'

As I sat drowsing at the kitchen table, opposite the courtyard window, I started thinking about things. The light in Concha's room was on and there were lights in the apartment where Tano lived too. As I said goodnight to my family where they sat huddled round the radio, as I kissed my grandmother, who was busy knitting, as I walked down the corridor and got undressed and looked out at the snowy street, I was, as my grandfather would have said, examining my conscience. The next day, I decided, I would tell Tano about Concha.

Tano came down when they had cleared away the snow from outside the front door. We made room for him on the kerb. He said he'd recovered from the wound to his head, that he knew who'd thrown the stone and was going to smash his face in.

'Who was it?' I asked.

'I'm going to smash his face in and then rub his chops in the dungheap in Campillo.'

He was talking to me as if I were just another member of the gang, rather than his special friend.

'But are you sure you know who did it? You might be wrong.'

He spat in the space between his feet, touched his bandage, and announced:

'This afternoon we're going sledging in Campillo Park.'

No one else had had the marvellous idea of sitting on a plank and sliding down the slopes over the grubby, packed-down snow. We were there until dark, going up and down, laughing as if nothing had changed. Tano and I returned home in silence and I was just about to tell him about Concha, when, for some mysterious reason, he mentioned her first.

'One of these days, we'll have to lie in wait for Concha.'

'Yes,' I said.

'It gets dark early now and we can catch her in the street. Then we'll shove her in the lift and go up to the top landing, where the door...'

'You mean the door onto the roof.'

We had planned this so often, and I wasn't to know that this would be the last time. We spent a really enjoyable evening and night together, talking about lots of things, like best friends.

I wasn't keen on the idea at all actually, and I was worried how Concha might react, but I went to call for him anyway, so that we could go and wait for her. He wasn't interested, though, and pretended to ignore me and made me go back upstairs with him to our apartment, so that Luisa could teach us some songs. It was Sunday afternoon, and a blustery wind was shaking the branches of the trees and blowing the ice off the tops of the barricades.

Luisa sat us down round the table and, after a while, we were joined by Rosita, who was only eight, and by her brother Joaquín, who, as everyone knew, had shown himself to be a real wimp when it came to stone-throwing fights. Tano's eyes shone each time he got to sing along with Luisa: '*Prietas las filas, recias, marciales...*'*—'In closed ranks, strong and martial...'.

'Now,' said Luisa, 'I'll teach you another really wonderful song. But don't sing too loudly.'

Then she cleared her throat and promptly started singing in a hoarse, brazen voice as if she were marching in a demonstration. '*Giovinezza, giovinezza, primavera di bellezza...*'

'That's great,' said Joaquín.

'What does it mean?'

'It's in Italian,' Luisa explained, 'because it's sung by the Italian youth movement. They're like our Nationalists, except they're Italians, from Italy.'

'And they wear black shirts,' said Tano.

'Exactly,' said Luisa.

Tano caught up with me in the hallway.

'Where are you going?'

* One of the songs of the Nationalist Youth League.

'Out,' I said as I made for the stairs. 'I don't want to sing songs like that.'

'We can go out later. Come back inside.'

'No! Besides, I can't stand that wimp, Joaquín, or Rosita or my sister, who's always pestering the life out of me anyway. I'm going to wait for Concha. I thought you wanted us to take Concha up onto the roof?'

'Come back here or I won't give you any more cigarettes,' he said, leaning on the banister as I went down the stairs. 'If you don't come back, I'll throw you out of the gang.'

'But I thought you wanted to ... Oh, get stuffed!'

The wind outside was so cold, I couldn't even cry.

At supper-time, everyone knew all about those black-shirted bastards and, even worse, someone had ratted on me and told them how I'd spent the whole afternoon out in the street. Riánsares was angry too and when I touched her thighs hoping we could at least quarrel and then make it up again, she didn't move, as if she were miles away, and, in the end, I got up and went to see my grandmother—the only one of the family who seemed halfway normal.

Tano didn't kick me out of the gang, mainly because he hardly spent any time with us now. He hung around with Joaquín and boys like him, as if he were otherwise occupied or found us boring. He was still the Leader, even though we often had fights with other gangs without him being there. Someone always told him what we'd been up to, so that he could give his approval or not, and he sometimes had really good ideas, and his soapbox car was still the best on the street.

With Concha, I never knew where I might find her—in the street, on the stairs, in Luisa's bedroom—nor whether she would let me touch her up a lot or a little, or if *she* would touch me or just send me packing, pretending to be shocked.

After Christmas, I asked Tano to give me back my Jules Verne books, which had been a present from my grandfather. He said he would, that he'd read them all anyway and would return them straight away. Later on, I discovered that he hadn't even read *The Children of Captain Grant*, which was the least boring of them. It took him a whole week to return them, and then only after I'd asked him again one night when we were trying to build a bonfire on an empty lot and he'd got angry with me. Perhaps I shouldn't have asked in front of the rest of the gang. I was upset and thought he'd forgotten. And then, on top of everything, there was that business between Riánsares and the fascist.

Most of my thoughts, however, were focussed on lying in constant wait for Concha. I was happy, although sometimes I would have odd thoughts, like when it occurred to me to wonder if Tano knew I was happy or imagined I was miserable. I think he did know I was happy. Or perhaps it never even crossed his mind, just as it had never even crossed mine that one day, the streets—the snow long since melted—would fill up with crowds of people and that priests would be seen out and about again, or that on the 'glorious morning' when Victory was declared, I would see Tano and Concha standing on the back of a lorry and singing that song about '*giovinezza*' or whatever it was, a song I didn't even know she knew.

Murder at the Atlantic

Guillermo Busutil

The refurbishment of our new apartment on the fourth floor of number 19 Gran Vía, took nine months and one week. It was a four-bedroom apartment with bathroom and kitchen, as well as three balconies with bowed wrought-iron balustrades. The building was known in Madrid as the Atlantic, that being the brand name of a well-known hot-and-cold-water dye, which gave ladies the promise of always having something new to wear, and its emblem was a star that crowned the city's night skyline.

When we finally moved in, what struck me most was the long street-level window full of photographs. The pale glow of a young beauty wearing a mantilla, the solemn legionnaire gazing heavenwards in a martial manner, the newly wed happiness of satiny couples in black and white, the large family lined up like a football team, the first communion of a boy in naval uniform, and the picture of an older man who seemed to be staring you coldly in the eye. 'That's Don José Botero', said my father, recognizing the chief inspector of police who had been a good friend of my late grandfather, a provincial judge. It occurred to me then that those faces, which seemed to be eyeing me with intense curiosity, were the equivalent of prying neighbours in that building separated by the Gran Vía from the crowded, fashionable Cafetería El Americano, where one could enjoy a Cinzano or a *café crème* Manhattan, and whose revolving door could easily catch your laggardly shadow by surprise.

Shortly afterwards, I learned that not only did those watching faces belong to some of the Atlantic's tenants, they were the work of Studio Akerman, located in the foyer with its polished chequered floor. This dark, glossy territory, always with a faint whiff of bleach about it, was ruled over by a gaunt, tetchy concierge who, most unusually, wore above her left breast an Iron Cross. This, apart from her widow's pension, was the only legacy left her by her husband, an officer in the Blue Division, who had died bravely in the far-off hellhole that was Russia. This was the same fiery hell to which the Sergeantess (as she was known) would have liked to dispatch Capote and his gang, whenever she caught them throwing lit matches into the green letter boxes on the mezzanine. This was just one of many acts of vandalism perpetrated by the gang, who presided over the local area and the site occupied by a half-demolished house adjoining the Gran Vía Cinema, where they showed double bills. The three remaining walls of the house were tattooed with scooped-out hearts and blotches, and we often came across the discarded butts of mentholated Piper cigarettes, extra-long Lolas, and Ducados unstained by lipstick. Anyway, at the time, my principal means of amusement before lunch was to read Zane Grey novels while seated outside Studio Akerman, from where I could also hear the news bulletin on National Radio emanating from the Sergeantess's apartment. This was the signal I was waiting for in order to ambush the ever-punctual Don José and be the first to shoot.

The game had been initiated by the inspector himself the very first time we met him on the landing of the main staircase, where he and my father stood chatting for a while. I was armed, that day, with a cap pistol, and he challenged me to see who was fastest on the draw. After that first encounter, we repeated our duel every day, with varying mortality rates. This greatly surprised the other residents, given the normally serious demeanour of that stern, heavily built gentleman, whose eyes had a threatening glint to them, similar in intensity to a reading lamp, and who was always impeccably dressed in a blue jacket and a small fedora worn slightly at an angle. This was the habitual plain-clothes uniform of a policeman known to take a tough line with the many swindlers, layabouts, and villains whose criminal activities he had put paid to. He had enjoyed a highly successful career to which he had devoted himself wholeheartedly, having no happy family to accompany him on life's journey. This deeply entrenched solitude would, according to my mother, weigh all the heavier when he reached retirement age, as he soon would, and it was perhaps this same solitude that caused him to bestow on me a degree of protective affection. And I had no hesitation in making use of that affection when Capote robbed me, variously, of three tops, two white marbles, and my favourite black whistle; on more than one occasion, he had even left me with bruises on my face, to which my mother would apply her soft Pond's cold-cream hands. After one such incident, the inspector promised that, if Capote continued to bother me, he would handcuff his hands behind his back and lock him up in a dungeon in Plaza de Los Lobos.

Our mutual ambushes fed that close complicity, indeed, my mother played an active role in this by telephoning Don José to tell him that she had just despatched me on an errand to the shop, thus giving him the opportunity to leap out at me from his hiding place, or, alternatively, she would warn me that the inspector had been spotted just a hundred yards from the house. Oblivious to the stares of passers-by, he and I would try to outdo each other by being fast enough on the draw with our index fingers and deadly enough with our aim to fatally wound our opponent, who would then pretend to fall down dead on Gran Vía itself or in one of the adjacent streets, while the winner would gleefully shout out a number and chalk up yet another victory. Even if I lost, Don José would give me a five-peseta piece and two *reales* so that I could continue practising throwing the coin in the air and getting my imaginary bullet through the little hole in the centre. Then he would smile at me and, still out of breath, immediately cross the road for a solitary assignation with a red martini in El Americano.

And so the months passd, until one lunchtime, on my way back from school, I saw Don José walking slowly towards me, looking grave and distracted. Before he could catch sight of me, I took shelter in the darkness of the doorway and, as soon as he appeared, silhouetted against the light, I shot him, crying: 'Straight through the heart.' Don José stopped dead in his tracks, pressed his hand to his chest and, looking at me with wide eyes, tottered slightly, before falling backwards onto the ground. He had never, I thought, feigned death better, as he lay there on his back, his hat having rolled away onto one black square of the chequered pavement. But he seemed not to hear what I was saying, while I waited for him to get to his feet with his usual smile and without that fixed look in his eyes, as if he were posing for a passport photo at Studio Akerman. Señor Akerman himself opened the door of his studio and, seeing Don José lying motionless in the doorway, sent me running to get my father. A crowd of anxious neighbours soon gathered, including Capote, who was staring at me in astonishment, impressed by my 'crime'; then two ambulance men arrived to carry Don José away from the foyer of the Atlantic, never to return.

The Atlantic is no longer crowned by the advertisement that once outshone Venus, nor does the Sergeantess still rule over the foyer, but whenever I go into the building, all these years later, I always remember the day I shot dead a policeman.

Luzmila

Álvaro Pombo

Luzmila was tall, thin, and very ordinary. She had proved
to be a good worker in her days as an errand girl for the
nuns, but long before the sparse, diffuse point at which
her earliest memories began, she had been at the beck and
call of swarms of errant people: her parents, who each
went their respective ways, her bedridden grandmother
reaching out to her with the blind, confident voracity of
all trapped creatures, her siblings, and, finally, the nuns,
who, unintentionally, but with the infallible egotism of
the angels, kept Luzmila with them for nine or ten years,
letting her believe that one day she would enter the convent as a novice—as a lay sister, which is what she wanted.
They sent her running back and forth on their footling
errands, only to declare at last that she had no 'true

vocation' and that, in the mother superior's words, 'she would be far better off working for a good family'.

'Dear Jesus, in whom I firmly believe,' Luzmila would whisper each night, lulling herself to sleep, 'it is for my sake that you are there on the altar, that you give your body and blood to the faithful soul as heavenly nourishment.' And Luzmila would repeat, in the same faint murmur as the choir of nuns at the Convent of the Most Pure Conception: 'To the faithful soul as heavenly nourishment.'

The nuns at the Convent of the Most Pure Conception were known as the 'Most Pures', partly because it was shorter and partly because the Holy Founding Mother, the Blessed María Antonia de Izarra y Vilaorante, devoted herself to saving girls from a life of licentiousness; and partly, too, because of the exquisite bobbin lace and embroidered sheets and tablecloths they produced. The girls from the 'Most Pures' slept in a blue-and-white painted dormitory in twelve identical beds, separated by six very rickety wardrobes, one for every two girls, and which were frequently broken into and the cause of many arguments. The sisters taught the girls to get up early, to mend clothes—using the invisible mending technique, almost like a spiritual emendation, which was the pride of the convent—to say, 'Yes, Madam,' 'No, Madam,' and 'As you wish, Madam,' and the brighter, keener girls were taught to cook the whitish stews that the nuns had invented (for purity, as they say, is in all things) and the recipe for *yemas de la Beata*—sweets made from egg yolk and butter—much sought-after by the pious ladies who tended to predominate in the area. And having thus equipped the girls, the convent would find positions for them later on as cooks and maids in the select households of families who regularly attended Nocturnal Adoration. The girls were fond of Luzmila because she would swap their novels for new ones, but among themselves, they all considered her to be both holier-than-thou and slightly crazy.

When Luzmila left the convent, the nuns found her a post as a nanny, and thus she began a long peregrination through houses and more houses, through jobs that always ended in the same way: when the children left primary school and began to dress themselves, her employers would tell Luzmila that she should start looking for another post.

And so Luzmila would start looking and sooner or later (usually sooner, because she was always given excellent references), she would find another post. Each time she left, she did so very early in the morning, when the refuse collectors could be heard up the street; she would say goodbye to the concierge, think fondly of the children she was leaving, then set off carrying her wooden suitcase.

Her hair was caught back in a thick, greying plait which she coiled up each morning in a bun at the back of her neck. She wore brown cotton stockings. She worked with eyes downcast. She spoke without raising her voice. She always had in her bag a pair of check slippers to wear around the house. She walked about the households where she was employed as she walked about the convent, never prying into anything, never looking at the pictures in the nuns' prayer books, never leafing through the master's newspaper before the master had read it, never filching food from the pantry. At the age of sixty-five, she ended up in Madrid, and since, by then, there was no demand for nannies, she found work as a cleaning woman.

Luzmila had saved a few thousand pesetas, and, wishing to avoid banks or savings banks, she always carried these with her in an envelope, along with the Infant Jesus's box. She had a very clear idea of the Kingdom of Heaven. It was—she firmly believed—the home of the Infant Jesus of Prague. And the Glory was like the six o'clock Benediction held by the Carmelites, only without the need to brave the indifferent evening rain, the penetrating solitude of the streets, or the walk past the assault guards posted at the door of the police station opposite the church. Luzmila never went to the cinema or read the newspapers or listened to the radio. With the years, and after all that travelling from one end of Spain to the other (because in her days as a nanny, Luzmila had travelled frequently from provincial capital to provincial capital), she had ceased to have a fixed church, that is, a fixed place where she could worship. Her family had dispersed years before, when her mother and her grandmother died, and Luzmila, who had loved her brothers and sisters dearly, could now barely remember them. Or, rather, she remembered only the dirty overalls, the Sunday suits hanging lifeless in the wardrobe, the sour smell, and the masculine disorder of her brothers' bedroom. Indeed, she remembered that disorder as a clear, enduring, oppressive, unpleasant fact. Perhaps, without her realizing, this was what had drawn her to the refined world of the convent and to the nuns, as pretty as pictures, with their firm, eternally young faces framed by their wimples. She found the unreal sayings and manners of the nuns as captivating as a fairy tale. And she wanted to be the lay sister who polished the parlour and kept the tiles in the corridors as bright and shining as a wall of mirrors.

The vagueness with which Luzmila recalled her own family was transformed over the years into a precise, detailed image of the Holy Family. St Joseph returning from the carpenter's shop in the evenings; the Virgin spinning or sewing some trousers for the Infant Jesus; the Infant Jesus eternally playing with the doves (which

were always white and of which there were always five).
Luzmila did not vary the movements of her characters very
much; on the contrary, the little they did, they did in the
same way and almost without moving. The mystery and the
charm of imagining something consists precisely in it being
tota simul et perfecta possessio*—and utterly motionless.

Luzmila took communion every day very early in the
morning and then went for a walk, killing time until nine
o'clock, when she would arrive at whatever household
currently employed her. To take communion is to eat
and drink the body and blood of the Infant Jesus of
Prague. Luzmila always found this idea slightly terrifying:
the sacred gruesomeness of the feast, the empty stomachs,
and the souls without a stain or fleck or particle of sin.
Luzmila made a point of removing her false teeth before
taking communion, reasoning that then she would not
risk biting the Holy Shepherd as he entered the fold, the
soft, sweet, pink, newly washed cave of her mouth. Luzmila had a horror of all those gaping mouths at the
communion rail, those gullets crammed with sacrilegious
teeth. In the end, the very thought of that sacrilege, of
biting the Holy Infant, provoked such anxiety in her that,
in order not to have to witness it, she began attending the
half-past-five mass in the church in Plaza de Manuel

---

* wholesome, simultaneous and perfect possession.

Becerra. In winter, Luzmila, still warm from her bed and from walking, would kneel down in the dark church which was—or so it seemed to her—entirely hers, and she would contemplate, enraptured, without praying or thinking, the bright butterfly flame of the lamp burning in the sacrarium and the devout, sour, composite smell of the church as it lay bathed in the submarine lightness of near-dawn that dazzled the figures in the stained-glass windows in the side chapels.

One day, the combined unreality of the deserted church and her own state of mind fused into one, and Luzmila found herself taking communion twice, in order to feel again the magical presence of that *panis angelicus*, the hard, bland, round wafer that tickled the palate and stuck to the cheek like an ice-cream cone. The next day, however, Luzmila felt that consuming two hosts one after the other demonstrated quite unprecedented greed, and so, when she returned to her pew, she pretended to cough and spat out the second host into her handkerchief. She felt uneasy all day, eager to finish work and get home in order to put the Infant away in a safe place. She kept looking at the handkerchief, although without daring to unfold it for fear that the defenceless wafer, the Infant Jesus, might catch cold. After work, she went into a haberdashery and bought a jewellery box, the biggest and best they had. It was decorated with enamelled shells and had a view of La Concha beach on the lid and an inscription that said: 'A souvenir of San Sebastián'. This sacrarium, this nest, gradually filled up with a collection of Infant Jesuses, and occasionally Luzmila saved both hosts, which began to warp and grow yellow from her dried saliva. It came to be Luzmila's reserve fund, far more real in its sheer unreality than the thousands of pesetas in the envelope. And it comforted Luzmila, as the impossible always comforts our impossible desires.

Luzmila lived in Madrid in an attic room with a right to use the kitchen. This 'right' meant that Luzmila could go down to the concierge's kitchen—on the landing below—'to warm up a bit of food'. From the very first day, though, it was clear that the concierge—who occupied a bedroom next to the said kitchen—had very particular views on what constituted a 'right'. She deemed that mere legality does not do justice to the real complexity of each individual case and that it was therefore wisest to temper the august impersonality of the law with a prudent application of her own law, enriching the concept of 'a right to use the kitchen' with the infinitely more subtle concept of being allowed to use it as a special favour. In this way, whenever a new tenant took up residence in the attic room, the concierge would give a little speech intended to impress on the new tenant that the only reason the 'right' remained in force was down to the concierge's peculiar goodness of heart (she had always been pretty right-wing, as any tenant could tell from the painting above her bed of the Sacred Heart of Jesus, adorned with a palm from Palm Sunday, and the photos of José Antonio and the Caudillo placed together, slightly askew, in a frame on top of the radio). Years had gone by since Luzmila last enjoyed the favour of using the kitchen. And this fact, along with everything else, disconnected the little of Luzmila that was still connected to the outside world. All that was left to her then was her professional identity, and she did her best to make herself a cleaning woman through and through, taking that role as far and as deep as necessary. This was the point at which Luzmila began to go so unnoticed in the world that the visible and the invisible met seamlessly in her.

A year after Luzmila's 'disappearance', the concierge was joined by a young niece from her village, the daughter of a younger sister, Rosa, who had died after being kicked by a mule (or by her husband, it was never quite clear). The niece had just turned twenty, although she could easily have passed for sixteen. Her name was Dorita, like the concierge, and she looked like a rather intelligent boy. It was precisely because she was intelligent and because she looked like a boy that she had got a job in the village working in an incubation shed. The wife of the owner would never have allowed a more alluring female anywhere near her husband, but Dorita was such a little slip of a thing that she slipped into the job at once, and that ability to slip into places became part of Dorita's character from that time on. Working with the incubators was an easy enough job (apart from the broken sleep), and a natural affinity immediately sprang up between Dorita (who had something strangely larva-like about her) and the hygrometric vicissitudes of the eggs lined up in their thousands on trays. Everything went well until an agricultural products representative appeared on the scene, a rather plump, slimy middle-aged fellow, who gave her a hundred pesetas and a packet of cigarettes for letting him get his leg over. From then on—although no one ever quite understood why—things went from bad to worse, and when her mother died after being kicked either by the mule or by her husband, Dorita came to live in her aunt's house in Madrid.

Dorita hung around the streets of Madrid thinking vaguely about getting a job and thinking rather more about *not* getting a job and simply enjoying seeing the sights. One day, in a cinema in Calle de Carretas, she met a man who rather resembled that agricultural products representative and, right there and then, she earned her second one hundred pesetas. And in pursuing that resemblance from cinema to cinema and from trick to trick, Dorita was soon left with no time to think, even vaguely, about finding a job. The men she picked up were always similarly gentle, paternal fellows, somewhat broad in the beam, who did not entirely understand themselves and invariably felt thoroughly ashamed when it was over. They always seemed frightened or lonely. They always said 'I can't give you very much', but nevertheless paid promptly the little they had promised at the start. Afterwards, they vanished without trace. This, among other things, was what made it the perfect job for Dorita. She would think proudly: 'The things that happen to me you wouldn't even read about in *El Caso*.' Dorita read *El Caso* every week, looking in vain for some case similar to her own. Dorita and her companions had a shared belief that theirs was the one invincible reality.

In that unreal, sourly picaresque Madrid, which covers the real Madrid like a second skin, Dorita spent her money like water on anything she saw, on the odd little things sold in the street, on bottles of nail varnish, of which she managed to collect hundreds. She still looked like the same Dorita of the incubators, except that now she had exchanged her overalls for a kind of loose shirt and trousers. When she wore trousers, she looked even more like an intelligent boy, and was occasionally pursued by queers, who mistook her for precisely that. Her aunt said of her that money simply slipped through her fingers, which was true, and in a sense, Dorita slipped through life as well; you barely saw her come and go. This fluidity would impregnate her entire existence. According to the concierge, it was an advantage having her in the house because 'she's sharp as a tack and brings in a bit of money too'. And Dorita did pay a weekly sum for bed and board. And to anyone who asked, her aunt would say: 'It's nice having a bit of company of an evening.' Dorita then became firmly established at her aunt's and was—to all appearances—learning to become a hairdresser at a salon in Calle de Atarazanas. This careful, exact lie had, as Dorita hoped, reassured her aunt completely.

Dorita and Luzmila met one night at the door of the lavatory. This was purely by chance, because they could easily never have met, and Luzmila's story doesn't depend on this meeting being anything other than accidental.

The lavatory gave onto a landing two steps down from Luzmila's attic room and three steps up from the concierge's kitchen. It was a high, narrow room, with a small window at roof height and a single, fly-spattered light bulb that appeared to be gazing down at its own reflection in the funereal toilet bowl. Luzmila was in the lavatory when the door handle turned from outside. She quickly got up to leave and mumbled an apology as she emerged, a tall, gaunt figure with her coat on over her long nightdress, not bothering to look to see who was there; and she would have walked straight past, but for Dorita, who was naturally sociable and who had, out of pure curiosity, attempted to approach Luzmila before. She grabbed Luzmila's arm and said: 'Sorry to rush you. I don't know what it was I ate, but it's given me the runs.' Luzmila went up to her room, feeling agitated and content. The following night, Dorita slipped into Luzmila's room and said: 'I just thought I'd pop in for a chat. I'm fed up to the back teeth with my aunt.' It then became the custom for Dorita to visit every night. And Luzmila grew accustomed to the custom, and the custom, as always happens, became a trap. Dorita would sit at the foot of the bed and chat away, interspersing her chatter with some of her adventures, enjoying watching her own life pass before her as she spoke. 'Don't get the wrong idea, I don't like sex at all,' she said. 'Some men want to plate you or grope you and others just want to tell you about their life, and some of them could talk the hind leg off a donkey, and then there was one guy who gave it to me very gently up the arse like a suppository, claiming he didn't know how to do it any other way. I tell you, horror movies have nothing on life.'

Dorita told these stories in the same tone of voice in which one recounts gossip or tittle-tattle, and Luzmila grew accustomed to them as well, although without entirely understanding them, much as we grow accustomed to our neighbours without ever understanding them.

Around that time, Luzmila suffered a mishap that made her life still narrower, were such a thing possible, and made her entirely dependent on the uncertain companionship of Dorita. Don Antonio, the priest, was known as 'el Comulguero' because all morning, every morning, at the chapel of Our Lady of Perpetual Succour, he gave communion every ten minutes. Wearing his stole and a rather creased half-chasuble that emphasized his stooped shoulders, he said mass early and then remained by the kneeler at the main altar. For this reason, there was always a long queue of communicants waiting for him, like the queue outside the butcher's. With practice, Don Antonio had developed both an abbreviated way of saying the *Corpus Domini Nostri*—reducing it to one word—and a series of conditioned reflexes that enabled him to leap up and offer communion as soon as he saw some vaguely human shape kneeling down before the altar of Our Lady of Perpetual Succour. Since Don Antonio reacted more to shape than face, it was easy for Luzmila to take communion along with everyone else at mass and then again, once or even twice, with Don Antonio. However, the time came for Don Antonio to retire, and he was replaced by a very earnest, learned, inquisitive priest, who was studying to be a canon and used every spare moment between masses, benedictions, confessions, novenas, and rosaries to prepare for his exam. He used to sit in one of the more central confessionals that was lit by a large light bulb, which made the little cabin resemble nothing so much as a puppet theatre, and in between studying his books and his index cards, he would observe his parishioners. He came to know them all, one by one, and since he had a naturally good memory and an eye for detail, he reached the stage where he had to make regular examinations of conscience, more like purges really, in order to wipe his mind clean of all the minuscule idiosyncrasies that he had, quite unwittingly, absorbed and remembered along with the articles of the *Summa Theologica*, and that he could not get out of his head. The gentleman with the grey hair who looked like a clerk at the Banco de Vizcaya; the wealthy lady who came to mass without her make-up on (God bless her) and who had said three rosaries in the time it took him to say the *lavabo* and read from the Gospel; the widow who spent the entire mass trying to find the words of the mass in the missal; the little girl in wellington boots; the young lad as handsome as St Stanislas, who piously attended mass every morning apart from Fridays and always knelt down before the Seventh Station of the Cross. And then there was that tall, rather stooped woman who took communion twice. The first time, he let it pass, thinking he must have been mistaken. The second time, however, he pounced on Luzmila like a devil. In her fright, Luzmila swallowed the second Infant Jesus and fled the church in terror, without hearing a word the priest was saying. Luzmila has never been seen twice by anyone and no one has ever taken a really good look at her. When the day comes and we hear no more of her, she will be neither more nor less invisible than before.

One evening, Luzmila arrived home early. When she tried to open the door and found it bolted from the inside, she began to shout. She pounded on the door and kept shouting, and eventually Dorita opened it. Luzmila went in and found a man hurriedly pulling on his clothes. He escaped, entangled in the jacket and raincoat he just had time to throw over his shoulders. Dorita ran after him. Luzmila sat down on the bed without removing her over-coat. The room was filled with the murmur of the urban dusk and the wild, yellowish, Castilian winter. She could see the greenish tiles of the roof very close to the head of her bed, like a precipice. Dorita did not come and see her for two whole weeks. And Luzmila's feelings were as disparate and confused as ants in an ants' nest. She grew thinner and seemed ever more sunk in herself, ever greyer. It's hard to say whether Luzmila was visibly losing colour, corporeality, being, or bulk. Maybe she wasn't even suffering, because for Luzmila, pain, perhaps, had the same tenacious structure of those material objects to whose inescapable weight we become accustomed from birth and which we do not even consider to be obstacles.

After those two weeks, a tearful Dorita returned, saying something about being in a terrible fix and how it had been the first and only time and how much she loved Luzmila. Dorita believed her own lie so completely that she wept bitterly, sobbing: 'Look, Luzmila, I'm crying,' as if to say that anyone who cries must have some good in them. This was a complete waste of time really, because, in Luzmila's mind, Dorita and the Infant Jesus of Prague were beyond judgement (our beliefs, after all, are the structures by which we judge real objects, whether possible or impossible). They were both part of the last strand of identity left to Luzmila. Besides, how could she judge Dorita's story when she barely heard it? The only thing she really saw and heard was that Dorita was asking forgiveness, although Luzmila didn't know why (because the incident that had occurred two weeks before was not connected causally in her imagination with the incident she was witnessing now). She had been greatly confused by Dorita's absence, not because it upset some particular plan or project of hers, but simply because she found it confusing. However, that feeling of pure confusion was immediately cancelled out by the pure objectless joy of having Dorita back, just as two quantitatively and qualitatively equal things cancel each other out. 'Forgive us our debts as we forgive our debtors.' Luzmila had always found those words surprising because she had never been able to work out who in the world her debtors could be. She didn't think anyone owed her anything. Neither debtors nor enemies can penetrate true solitude. Only the enmity that knows no enemies and the offence that has no guilty parties can enter therein. Luzmila, then, felt no need to forgive Dorita. Indeed, on that occasion, she gave her three hundred pesetas, and that afforded Dorita her first glimpse of the envelope stuffed with banknotes. So taken aback was she that Luzmila's room seemed to fill with a kind of bent-backed silence and the showers of dust in the room shone like snowfalls of ghostly pins.

When Luzmila went to the lavatory the following night, Dorita took another two hundred pesetas, and for the first time, she experienced shame, the shame that, for everyone apart from Dorita herself, would later become shamelessness. And out of that shame was born, like a good feeling, or, rather, an easy and immediate feeling, the idea of compensating Luzmila in some way, because, in the imbalance that follows a fall, the idea of compensating someone is always instantly present, as a possibility. And so to compensate Luzmila for the theft, Dorita began to trace on Luzmila's unsatiated skin and need for tenderness the ambiguous lines of love. It was like a bad performance at a puppet show. But every evening, Luzmila would return home thinking joyfully of Dorita's sweet, moist body. And in Luzmila's dreams and dozings, Dorita became

the Infant Jesus—well, an incarnation is an incarnation—
sleeping, exhausted, in the Infant Jesus's box along with the
other crumbling hosts. In Dorita's imitation of love, cruelty
lurked, with its tiny translucent suckers. For two weeks,
possibly longer, Luzmila experienced the accelerated pulse
of blood threading the oblique needles of a late, empty
spring. Sexuality adds nothing to an interpersonal relationship that is not already contained in the mere concept of
that relationship. What it adds (and which is not contained
in the concept) is a meaningless animation, a somnambular
acceleration, the ultimate snare. During that time, Luzmila's pious imaginings became keener, more perfect, and
more absurd than usual. She even started talking about
them to herself in the street and, when she got home, she
would describe them to Dorita.

'Once, the Infant Jesus wouldn't go to sleep,' she said,
'and even though they held him and rocked him, he just
wouldn't go to sleep, talking all the time about the Passion
and how painful the crown of thorns would be. Then the
swallows came and plucked out the nails.'

And she was assailed again and again by the same
image: the Infant Jesus, plump and fair, so unlike the
children of her siblings, who, having been born in the
years of shortages, were old before their time, bow-legged,
irritable, and crotchety, and with greenish-yellow skin,
like the colour of the bread then. It was different with

the Infant Jesus, who began life with the Annunciation and with the Angel's clear words, with the moon beneath his feet and a crown of twelve stars about his head. The Virgin lived in a clean street in a little white house with green doors neatly painted by St Joseph. The windows were decorated with pots of geraniums, and there was a garden at the back, with marble columns holding up the porch, and a marble fountain in the same colour with a little spout of water that never ran dry. The Virgin kept everything spotless. At the bottom of the garden were some pear trees that bore ripe pears all year round, and a bed of maize with cobs whose glowing red-gold kernels the Infant Jesus husked each evening.

These stories alarmed Dorita. 'She's a bit cracked,' she thought to herself, and this thought reassured her in the sense that one need not treat a mad person with the same consideration as one would someone normal. A mad-woman is, after all, a joke, like the village idiot, sometimes petted and sometimes beaten. Initially, Dorita found the stories amusing, but then she got fed up with them. One night, after they had recited 'Dear little Baby Jesus', the prayer Luzmila had taught Dorita, and once Luzmila had fallen asleep, exhausted, Dorita shot out of bed like an arrow, opened Luzmila's bag, and made off with the enve-lope. When Luzmila woke the next morning and went to put the Infant Jesus's box next to the envelope as she did every day, she found the envelope missing. Carefully, calmly, she searched the room, as one might search for a lost thimble; there were not many things in the room and Luzmila inspected them all, one by one, like someone checking a very simple sum. She experienced a slight dizziness that resembled the emptiness of life in that it was entirely smooth, in that it did not hurt or cause anguish or anxiety in any precise sense, in that it had no causal connection with any event past or future. The only thing Luzmila did not do—as if she had suddenly broken the habit of a lifetime—was go to work that morning. Instead, she walked the streets and, in Plaza de Manuel Becerra, went into the dusty provincial park behind the church, where she sat down on a bench and remained there, motionless, for several hours. Then she felt a need to urinate and walked up Calle de Alcalá to the Retiro Park, where she knew she would find some public toilets. Then she walked very slowly back to Manuel Becerra. Then she went home and slept until the next day. And the following morning, she began again or continued as usual, as a cleaning woman. And she put away more than half her wages in an envelope that she kept alongside the Infant Jesus's box.

The Ballad of the River Manzanares

Ignacio Aldecoa

From the west to the south stretch long needles of cloy-
ingly purple clouds. From the west to the north lies the
mild blue of evening. To the east are the pale façades,
the cavernous spaces, the phosphorescent blackness of
the storm and the advancing night. High up, in the distance, like a curve of white beach, hangs the half-moon.

A thin, cold, sad wind blows in from the nearby fields.
The smoke from the trains, the smoke from the bonfires of
dry leaves, the humble smoke from the shacks built along the
right bank, all sully the otherwise crystalline evening. Bats

flitter, high-pitched, wings beating, along the river's course. The trees are a floating, misty green. The Manzanares grows smooth and opaque, like one long, lustreless thread. The irritating loudspeaker from the last open-air café, the last café of autumn, never ceases to blare forth, is never silent. Over the black hills of the Casa de Campo, a plane hovers in the western sky, now tinged greenish-yellow.

From the repair shops and the factories, the workers are walking back into the city. They move with the weary flow of a large river that will vanish into the urban labyrinths until the bitter, inhospitable, morning reflux.

Gas lamps. Beneath the leafy glow of the street lamp someone is waiting. The lamps make the evening shapes less distinct, make the permanent flashlight of the half-moon more distant, the shadows in the woods deeper. Beneath the lamp the waiting is over.

'Hi, Pilar.'

'Hi, Manuel.'

'Shall we go, Pilar?'

'Yes, Manuel.'

'Shall we go to the station, Pilar?'

'Wherever you like, Manuel.'

'Do you fancy a drink, Pilar?'

'Just a coffee for me, Manuel.'

'OK, a coffee for you, Pilar, and for me ...'

'For you a drink, Manuel.'

'In Bar Narcea, Pilar?'

'The Cubero's better, Manuel.'

'The coffee's better in the Narcea, Pilar.'

'They give you more tapas with your drink in the Cubero, Manuel.'

'You're looking very pretty, Pilar.'

'Am I, Manuel?'

'Yes, Pilar.'

'Do you like me, Manuel?'

'Yes, Pili.'

'Good, Manolo, because I love you.'

'A lot, Pili?'

'Oh, yes, a lot, Manolo. How about you?'

'I love you a lot too, Pili.'

Manuel the railway worker shivers. He asks:

'Shall we go, Pilar?'

'All right, Manuel.'

Lovers enjoy saying each other's names, just as bosses enjoy saying people's surnames. The man in charge of the Estación del Norte tram stop is issuing orders. He shouts at the conductor on the Campamento tram:

'González, change the trolley and be quick about it! González, pass me the logbook! Did you hear me, González?'

He shouts at the driver of the Campamento tram:

'You're five minutes late, Rodero! You've got to catch up, Rodero! Get a move on, Rodero!'

He shouts at the old linesman:

'Wake up, Muñoz! Come on, Muñoz, watch out for number 60!'

Soldiers skid on the metal studs on their boots as they rush into the metro. The young matchgirl screams at the top of her voice:

'Disgusting creatures! Donkeys!'

The chestnut-seller joins in:

'They're like animals, they are.'

The blind man shakes his head and cries:

'Get your lottery tickets here!'

From her kiosk, the newsagent casts a bored eye over life and tells a customer:

'We've sold out of *Marca*.'

Pilar and Manuel have walked past the bar with the good coffee and the one that serves most tapas. They go into the Revertito instead. They squabble a little, as is only right. That's what love is like.

'Why have you got to be home by eight, Pilar?'

'I've told you why three times already, Manuel.'

Manuel gets all contrary, because that's part of the game.

'Well, it's just doesn't wash with me, Pilar.'

Pilar pretends to get upset, because she knows she has to.

'Oh, Manuel, honestly!'

Manuel falls silent, and Pilar insists:

'My mother told me ...'

'Your mother...'

'Until we get married, my mother's the boss.'

'Maybe we won't get married.'

Pilar falls silent, her eyes shining. Manuel grows bolder.

'I mean, the way things are, maybe we won't get married ...'

Pilar says nothing. Manuel goes on:

'... because I'm just about up to here with it, I've had enough ...'

Pilar fixes her gaze on the mirror behind the bar. Manuel goes too far.

'No, really, I could walk away now and forget all about you and your wretched excuses.'

This time, Pilar reacts. She draws herself up, proud, dignified, superior.

'I'm getting pretty tired of it myself. Just say the word and we'll drop it. You can leave, if you like, but it'll be for good, mind, no coming back. For good, you understand?'

Manuel decides that the best response, the most manly response, is to order another drink.

'Another drink, please.'

Pilar is tapping her foot, apparently distracted, staring out through the windows at the street. Manuel makes an attempt at irony.

'You in a hurry, then?'

Pilar's tapping grows faster.

'You know I am.'

'Your mother, eh?'

Pilar pulls a face, presses her lips together, then says:

'So, are you going or staying?'

It's dark now. The fat storm clouds have spread southwards. Manuel has unzipped his leather jacket, because the drink has made him hot. Pilar is walking beside him, not saying a word. Manuel is whistling.

It's dark now. The lightning gets swallowed up by the plain. The changing-over of the trams creates its own lightning. The boss is busy talking to the guard in charge of the trams leaving the station. A long line of soldiers is waiting for the Campamento tram. The young matchgirl is flirting with a soldier. He says:

'I'll take you to the cinema, if you like.'

The matchgirl purses her lips.

'I'm not the cinema type.'

'If you say so, sweetheart.'

'Do you really think I'd go to the cinema with an infant like you? Come off it!'

The soldier is momentarily put out, but he quickly recovers.

'Come on, I know you.'

'You know me? Get away!'

A friend of the soldier shouts to him from the long queue for the tram.

'Hurry up, Luis, or you'll miss it.'

Emboldened by their imminent farewell, Luis says:

'I'll come and pick you up tomorrow, darling.'

'Oh, go fry an egg!'

'I'll take you to the cinema or anywhere else you want to go.'

'You couldn't afford to take me where I want to go.'

'See you tomorrow, sweetheart.'

Luis runs for the tram. The matchgirl attends to a customer.

'It's one peseta for five.'

'I'll have five then.'

It's dark now. Before they reach the Glorieta de San Antonio, Manuel buys some peanuts from a stall that also sells fruit, chips, gherkins, and shoelaces. It's rather nice to think how cosy it would be sitting at the stall, chatting to your girlfriend, warming your feet on a brazier, and eating peanuts.

'Do you want a peanut, Pili?'

Manuel is slowly softening. Pilar does not reply.

'Come on, Pili, I bought them for you because I know you like them.'

Drink has made him sentimental.

'Don't be daft, Pili. Eat one, just one, so that I can see you're not still angry with me.'

Manuel takes her arm. Pilar is walking coldly and gravely along.

'I love you, Pili.'

Silence.

'I'm asking you to forgive me, Pili. Will you?'

Pilar says:

'There's nothing to forgive, Manuel.'

'Yes, there is, Pili. Do you forgive me?'

'I forgive you, Manuel.'

Pilar's hand seeks Manuel's hand. He squeezes it tightly.

'It's just that you're so ... You seem to enjoy making me suffer.'

'But it's all forgotten now, right, Pili?'

'Yes, Manolo, it's all forgotten, but you're so ...'

'Would you like a peanut, Pili?'

'Yes, please, Manolo.'

'Shall I peel it for you, Pili?'

'If you like, Manolo.'

'Let go of my hand for a moment, then, Pili.'

Manuel puts the peanuts in her mouth.

'More?'

'No, Manolo, I'll choke.'

On the path by the river, the shadows of the trees form a tunnel. Along the Manzanares sails the deep, hesitant, phosphorescent half-moon. In the distance, upriver somewhere, a dog is barking.

'What if we were to drown together, Pili?'

'I wouldn't mind if we both went together. I wouldn't mind drowning with you.'

'Pili ...'

Manuel pauses.

'Pili, do you want to talk about us?'

'Yes, Manolo.'

'Let's get married before Christmas.'

'Whatever you say, Manolo.'

The dog is still barking; at the moon, at the darkness, at love. The clouds have spread from the south to the west.

'Let's go back into the light, Manolo.'

The murmur of the river fades.

'Let's go back into the light, Manolo.'

'Pili ...'

'Come on, Manolo.'

'OK.'

In the night, upriver, the dog has stopped barking. The moon sails across the open sky behind the clouds. The waters of the Manzanares are now pitch-black.

A Clear Conscience

Carmen Martín Gaite

'I keep telling you not to take it personally. I do, Luisa, I tell her all the time. He works too hard. He's tired, that's all. It's hardly surprising, really. He's just exhausted. Look, at least have a cup of tea.'

These last words coincided with the phone ringing. Mariano went to answer it. He hadn't yet taken off his raincoat.

'It is a very unforgiving profession,' said Aunt Luisa.

'Hello.'

'... and then there's his heart condition too.'

'I'm sorry? I can't hear. Can you be quiet a moment, Mama. Who's speaking?'

The voice at the other end was very faint, drowned out by a confusion of noises, as if trying to make its way past many barriers.

'Is Dr Valle there?'

'Yes, speaking. Can you speak up? I can barely hear you. Who is this?'

Mila was standing almost wedged into the corner, underneath the shelves crowded with liqueur bottles, her back turned to the men in the bar. She pressed her lips to the phone.

'Hello, is that you, Dr Valle?'

'Yes. Who is this?'

She took a few moments to answer; she found it easier to talk with her eyes closed. She was gripping the black receiver hard, and her hands were sweating.

'I don't know if you remember me, but my name's Milagros Quesada, from the clinic in San Francisco de Oña,' she blurted out.

'How often do I have to tell you? Call your local GP. Why ring me up at this hour? Isn't there a GP you can call?'

'Yes, sir.'

'So why are you calling me?'

'He says my little girl is dying, that he won't see her again because there's no point.'

'And what do you want me to do?'

'He doesn't understand. You made her better last year, don't you remember? A little eight-year-old girl, fair-haired, you must remember, she was almost as ill then as she is now. She had something wrong with her ears. I can pay whatever you normally charge.'

'But who gave you my phone number? Sister María?'

'No, sir. It's on a prescription I kept from your last visit. The other doctor doesn't understand what's wrong with her, and if you don't come, she'll die. She took a real turn for the worse this afternoon. It frightened me to see her like that. She's dying and ...'

She kept shifting her weight from one leg to the other as she talked, still with her back turned on the men in the bar, still wedged into the corner, as if pressed up against the grille of a confessional. A young man in a blue safari jacket, who had the look of a taxi driver, was hypnotized by her swaying buttocks. Another man said: 'Shut up, will you, Príncipe Gitano's on the radio.' And someone turned up the volume. Mila started to cry, her forehead resting on the tiled wall. The doctor's voice was saying:

'Yes, yes, I understand, but it's always the same. People call me at the last moment, when there's nothing more to be done. If the other doctor said he can't do anything, that isn't because he doesn't understand. I'll just say the same. Don't you see? Don't you see that if everyone did what you're doing now, I'd have to move to Puente de Vallecas permanently? I have my own patients to deal with, and I can't see everyone.'

'... little golden rose, little rose of Jericho,' shrilled the radio immediately above her. Mila covered her free ear.

'But I'll pay you, I'll pay you,' she begged falteringly. And a tear slipped through the holes in the earpiece and possibly onto the doctor's face, because he suddenly adopted a bored, routine tone: 'Look, don't cry, I'll see if I can fit you in first thing tomorrow morning' and perhaps he said something else as well, but she experienced those words, so disconnected from her and her problem, like a slap in the face.

'What do you mean "tomorrow"?' she said, almost shouting. 'I'm telling you she's dying. Don't you understand? I said I'd pay the same as one of your private patients. It has to be now, you have to come and see her now. If one of your paying patients called you, you wouldn't be asking her for explanations, would you?'

Mariano couldn't help but smile. He glanced at his watch. She went on:

'Well, it's the same with me. Don't worry, I'll find the money somehow.'

'That's not the point. Don't talk nonsense.'

'I'm not talking nonsense!' Mila retorted.

However, her voice immediately grew depressed again.

'Forgive me, I don't know what I'm saying. Please come.'

'All right. Where are you?'

It was ten to eight. He would have time to warn Isabel. She wouldn't like it, but this was sure to be a simple case, easily resolved. He'd say: 'I won't be long, my love. Make yourself pretty. I'll be back in no time.'

'Chabolas de la Paloma, number 5.'

'What, before the petrol station?'

'No, you keep straight on at the crossroads, then, further on, take a left...but, wait, I'll tell you what, will you be here soon?'

'In about twenty minutes, that's how long it takes by car.'

'Well, I'm calling you from the bar on the opposite corner from the petrol station. I'll wait for you here and then I can direct you. Because if you don't remember where the house is, you'll get lost.'

'OK, fine.'

'I'm in the bar opposite the petrol station, right?'

'Something to do with money,' thought the man in the blue safari jacket. With the radio blasting out, he had only managed to catch her last few words, when she was talking more loudly; he watched her pause with the receiver still in her hand, like the empty sleeve of a jacket, then replace it unhurriedly on the cradle and turn to reveal a flushed,

slightly tear-stained face. God, she's pretty. Probably a lovers'
spat. He's put the phone down on her. Gorgeous figure too!
Now she was moving away from the bar. 'Thanks, Señor
Julián,' she said to the barman, who didn't even look at her;
then she stood for a moment in the middle of the room,
hesitating, staring out at the street through the rectangle of
the door. There was a different light out there, shading
from dark into bright. A thin rain had begun to fall; there
must be a rainbow somewhere; and suddenly there was a
crowd of people milling round the cigarette machine,
girls in brightly coloured cardigans. There was a table
next to the first window, and the waiter was wiping it
with a damp cloth.

'Can I get you anything?'

She sat down. Her legs felt weak, and she still had the
echoing sound of the phone inside her head.

'Yes, a glass of red wine, please.'

The petrol station was just opposite. It was a good
place to wait.

'Hello, sweetheart, do you mind if I keep you
company?'

She glanced up at the man leaning his hands on the
marble tabletop. She didn't know him. She shrugged and
continued to gaze out of the window. The man in the blue
safari jacket sat down.

'Bring my bottle over from the bar, will you, and two glasses,' he said to the waiter. 'Will you let me buy you a drink, love?'

She looked down at the table. She had a few grey hairs. She said:

'If you like.'

Twenty minutes by car, he had said. It was better to have a bit of company than sit there alone. Anything was better than being alone. She needed a drink, especially after the impudent way she'd spoken to the doctor. She drank the first glass down in one. The man sitting opposite was studying her curiously.

'What's your name?'

'Mila. Milagros.'

'That's a nice name. Here, have some more wine.'

He felt intimidated for some reason, which was ridiculous when it was all going so smoothly. She never took her eyes off the rain and the blue-painted petrol station.

'What are you thinking about, sweetheart?'

'Nothing. Choose an answer: Yes or No.'

'Yes, of course, yes. I could only ever say "Yes" to you.'

He had said 'Yes'. He had said it three times. Andrea was going to die. And yet she didn't want to cry, she wasn't unhappy, as if someone else were feeling all her pain. After three nights without sleep, she was exhausted. The wine made her warm and drowsy.

'You're not very chatty, Milagros. Say something.'

'I'm tired. I don't feel like talking.'

'Tired? Work's the only thing that makes a person tired.'

'Exactly.'

'So what work do you do? I wouldn't have thought you needed to work.'

'Well, I do.'

'With a face and a figure like yours, I mean.'

'I only have two options in this part of town. Either scrubbing floors or the other thing.'

'So you scrub floors?'

'For the moment, yes. God, look at that rain.'

The thin September rain had become a downpour. In Atocha, it formed an aggressive curtain of water, falling so hard and fast that Mariano almost had to stop the car. Then he gradually accelerated again. The wipers flicked aside the raindrops, which then gathered on the glass to form rivulets of water. On the radio they were playing a song that had been popular in summer. Mariano was keeping time, clicking his tongue and moving his head from side to side. He thought about Isabel, about the last few golden August days they had spent together in Fuenterrabía. Isabel in a swimsuit on the yacht; Isabel in evening dress and wearing that sleeveless white sweater and that coat. He yawned. It would soon be winter again.

Before him lay Avenida del Pacífico, louche and malodorous, with its rows of run-down houses. He reached Puente de Vallecas and continued straight on. The rain had eased now; people were gathering around the entrance to the metro and the cinema where a vast painted image of Marilyn Monroe stood out like a figurehead. He was nearly at the outskirts of the city, at the point where it disintegrates and bifurcates. He headed uphill, where the houses along the main road still clung on to a certain discreet dignity, but emerging from every side street were men and women whom he knew on sight; he knew their caves and their lairs; he knew that their shoes were letting in water and would still be letting in water come December. He knew, too, that there were many of them, whole swarms, and that they multiplied with each passing day, migrated from other poorer areas and grew in numbers, inhabiting earth and adobe dwellings that lay hidden behind the main street, like a contagion. Occasionally, they came out. There were so many of them that they could march on the heart of the city, invade it, contaminate it. Mariano turned off the radio. The people from the side streets watched him drive past in his car. Some stood still, hands in their pockets. He thought: 'They're getting ready. They'll start walking towards me now and corner me. Like in a Western. Like in *High Noon*.' Then he got out a cigarette and lit it with his left hand.

'God, I'm stupid,' he said, exhaling smoke. 'Especially seeing as I've cured most of them of something or other.'

He drew up next to the petrol station. At first, he saw no one there, then the door of the bar was flung open and a girl came running over to him, clutching her cardigan tightly about her. She turned round halfway to say something to a man who had followed her out. The man caught up with her, tried to grab her arm, but she pulled away and ran to the car, where Mariano leaned across to open the passenger door for her.

'Get in.'

'In the front with you?'

'Yes, of course. Is it far?'

The man was staring at them in amazement. He had come a little closer. As Mariano set off, he heard the man say:

'Bloody hell, girl, you're doing all right for yourself.'

But neither Mariano nor the girl looked at him.

'Very far? No, sir. It's the second on the left.'

'How's the patient?'

'I don't know. I was waiting for you, so I haven't been back. I left her with a neighbour.'

'What about your parents?'

'The little girl isn't my sister, she's my daughter.'

'And the father?'

'I've no idea. He's in Jaén or somewhere.'

Mariano turned to look at Mila. She had her head bowed and seemed lost in contemplation of her own hands, which lay on her lap, fingers interlaced. She was wearing a flowery skirt.

'Now I remember. You were ill yourself last year, weren't you? Or was it the year before? Didn't you have some fluid on your lungs?'

'Yes, sir. I'm sorry I was a bit short with you on the phone.'

She hadn't raised her head. She was now studying the nickel-plated knobs, the clock, the mileometer.

'Don't be silly. Do I turn off here?'

'Yes, here.'

They passed the coalyard and the last low houses. They entered open countryside.

'And you're better now?'

'Oh, yes. I don't get tired like I used to.'

'Drop by the clinic one morning anyway, so that I can X-ray your chest.'

'All right. The house is just round the corner. You'll have to leave the car here though.'

There were no houses in sight. They parked on the road. A dog was standing on a pile of rubbish, watching them. They walked along a dirt track. The rain, in the form of a brown liquid, was streaming down some steps worn concave with use. Below, a few small children were collecting the liquid mud in empty tin cans. They didn't bother to move out of the way.

'Get off, Rosen,' said the girl, kicking one of her companions.

'Look, Mila, hot chocolate,' said the boy, showing her his mud-smeared hands.

At the bottom of the steps was a kind of hollow surrounded by doors cut out of the ground, unevenly distributed along narrow alleyways. The light was fading. The whitewashed walls glowed in the encroaching gloom.

'Be careful where you put your feet,' the girl warned Mariano. 'As soon as there's a bit of rain, the whole place turns to mud.' Then she went on ahead of him and drew back the curtain covering one of the doors. Mariano stumbled over a pot of geraniums.

'Just a minute. OK, you can come in now.'

Inside, a shadowy shape got to its feet.

'How is she, Antonia?'

'Worse, I think. She's started getting delirious. Have you brought the doctor?'

'Yes. Turn on the lamp so that he can see. Come in, Doctor. She's here.'

By the light of the lamp, he saw a small stove and, to the right, the bed in which the little girl was lying. She was fair-haired, and her skin had a greenish tinge to it. She was breathing loudly. They went over to her.

'Let's see now. Sit her up.'

'Look, Andrea, it's the man who made you better last time.'

The little girl half-opened two very pale eyes and said:

'More than you ... more than anyone. All in gold.'

'There's another pillow if you need one.'

'Hold on to her, that's it. Support her back.'

The little girl struggled. She was panting.

'It's frightening. Bang ... bang.'

'Keep still now, keep still.'

More women came to the door. They started whispering among themselves. The neighbour who had been watching over the girl joined them.

'Be quiet. The doctor gets angry when people talk, he takes his work very seriously.'

'I know. He's the one who got my husband better. What does he say?'

'I don't know, he hasn't said anything yet. He's checking her ears. I don't know why. She's half-dead as it is.'

'Poor little thing.'

'Better dead than starving.'

'I know, it's hard to know what's for the best.'

Mila kept absolutely still, holding the lamp.

Mariano looked up at her illuminated face, then went over to the dim light of the door. She followed him.

'You say she had the last injection of streptomycin at five?'

'Yes, sir.'

'Do you want to wash your hands?' asked the neighbour, who had come back in and was standing a little apart.

'No, it's all right. You say you have no parents, no relatives.'

Mila started crying. The faces of the other women reappeared at the door.

'I have an aunt in Ventas, but we're not in touch. Is she going to die, Doctor?'

'She's gravely ill. She needs an operation on the brain, but it's very risky. If she can be operated on immediately, there's some hope she might survive. It's up to you. I can take you to the hospital in my car.'

'I don't know what to do. Please, tell me what I should do.'

'What more can I say? I've told you all I know. If you leave her here, she'll die for sure.'

'Let's go,' said Mila.

Mariano glanced at his watch.

'Come on then. Put a coat round her. Don't bother getting her dressed properly.'

Mila's hands were shaking. She had uncovered the little girl's thin body and was trying to put some socks on her.

'That blanket over there will do.'

The neighbour approached, holding the blanket, and said:

'Of course, she might die in the hospital too.'

The child's breathing had grown hoarse. Her skin was scalding hot to the touch. Mila raised a face disfigured with grief.

'What difference does it make if she dies in the hospital or here. Surely she'd be better off there, wouldn't she? You heard the doctor, if she stays here, she'll die anyway.'

She wrapped the child in the blanket and picked her up.

'Give her to me. I'll help you.'

'No, no, leave me.'

'Bring an umbrella or something. Quick.'

A woman brought one from her house. A very large grey umbrella. She opened it behind Mila. They went out. It was raining hard. The neighbours who were gathered at the door made way for them, then followed behind. Andrea's face was visible above Mila's shoulder: a pale smudge in the shadow of the umbrella.

'Poor little thing.'

'You can almost see the whites of her eyes.'

The doctor hurried on ahead up the steps to open the car door. The children who had been playing there before had gone. It was scarcely possible to make out the faces of the women following the cortège. Mila had stopped crying.

She laid the child down on the back seat, and got in next to her, with the child's head on her lap.

'Do you want me to go with you?' asked Antonia, peering in.

'No, thank you, I'll go on my own. I'll be all right.'

The door closed. It was very dark inside the car.

'Isn't this nice, Andrea, travelling in a car,' she said bending over the child, who was quiet now.

Mariano started the engine, and the women stood at the top of the steps, waving. When they drove out onto the main road, the street lamps were lit, and away in the distance, beyond the hill, they could see the purple haze of Madrid, the neon signs and the shapes of the tall buildings against the leaden sky. They drove past the bar opposite the petrol station.

'Drive fast,' Mila said to him. 'Will they be able to operate at once?'

'I hope so. I have to say, you're being very brave.'

The child was quite calm now. Mila didn't dare look at her or change position and remove her hand from the child's cheek.

'No, not really,' she said in a faint voice.

Then she closed her eyes and leaned back a little. She felt slightly queasy from the wine she had drunk earlier; her legs were so weak she could barely feel them. Sitting like that, with her head back, aware of the weight of Andrea's body on her lap, she felt suddenly quite calm. If she opened her eyes, she could see the street lamps and the doctor's shoulders. How comfortable she felt. It was nearly dark. The doctor was taking them out for a drive. A very long drive to somewhere far, far away. Andrea really liked cars. The doctor was driving and taking them where they needed to go. She didn't have to do or think anything. The worst thing was when you had to make decisions and people pestered you to sort matters out on your own. Not now though. Now she just had to let herself be driven along the streets.

She suddenly opened her eyes. A pedestrian crossing. The brakes jammed on. The car filled up with bright lights. Mariano turned his head.

'How's our patient?'

And then he saw Mila's face and her terrified eyes staring at him. She was sitting absolutely rigid, her hands in the air.

'You look, will you,' she said in a choked voice. 'I daren't. I daren't look at her. You look and tell me. I don't even want to touch her. I can't. I can't!'

Seized by a terrible trembling, she turned her head to the window, as if trying to avoid all contact with that other body. She was biting her thumbnails. Beside them, waiting for the lights to change, was another car, inside of which sat a black poodle, watching her, its nose pressed against the glass.

'Just tell me the truth,' she begged, almost shouting.

Mariano turned and knelt on the driver's seat. He saw the child's lifeless face, the blank eyes fixed on the roof of the car. He reached out to touch her. Mila had begun sobbing convulsively and the shuddering movements of her legs made the dead face move too. Mariano closed the child's eyes and pulled the blanket up to cover her. He folded down the back of the front passenger seat.

'There's nothing we can do now. I'm sorry. Come and sit in the front with me. I'll drive you back. Please. We can't stop here for long.'

Mila jumped into the front seat. She was shaking violently. She clung to Mariano and buried her face in his chest. He could feel her clinging frantically to him, imprisoning him; he was aware of her body under the thin blouse. The other cars started to move off. He tried to free himself.

'Come on now. Try and pull yourself together.'

'My daughter. Don't let her fall on the floor, will you?'

She stammered as she spoke, refusing to remove her head from its hiding place. Her whole body shook with her sobs.

'Don't you worry about anything. I'll drive you home. I'll get your daughter out of the car. I'll do everything. But let me go. I can't drive like this.'

Mila drew back, her face distraught, but she still grabbed his arm, even though he was now driving.

'No, don't take me home. It's dark now. No, please, don't take me home, I couldn't bear it. Take me somewhere else, anywhere.'

'But where? Don't talk nonsense. We have to take the child home. You're getting me worried now.'

'That's precisely it. I don't want to be alone with her tonight. I don't want to see her. I never want to see her again. I won't go home! We can leave her at the morgue or wherever, and you can take me somewhere else.'

She had hold of his right sleeve and was kissing it, smearing it with tears and lipstick. Her teeth were chattering.

Mariano placed his hand on her shoulder for a moment.

'Calm down. You won't be alone at home. Your neighbours know you and will keep you company. Please. I'll have an accident if we're not careful.'

They had turned round now and were heading back in the direction from which they had come.

'No. Not home. There's no one there I care about. I have no one. How can I go back to that house? Take me with you.'

'With me? Where?'

'You must have somewhere you can put me up. You've probably got a big apartment. Even if it's just for one night. Sit me in a chair and I'll be fine. I'll explain things to your wife or your mother or whoever. It'll only be until tomorrow. And tomorrow, who knows, they might decide to take me on as a maid.'

Mariano continued driving straight on. His eyes were fixed on the road, but he knew Mila was watching him, wanting to know what he would decide; and there he was, unable to say a word.

'Look, I understand what you must be going through,' he said at last, 'but you must trust what I say, because you're not yourself right now. Your neighbours care about you. I saw that this evening. Believe me, going home is the best and most reasonable thing to do.'

In the same rebellious tone she had used on the phone earlier, Mila said:

'You say you understand, but how can you? You haven't the faintest idea what I'm going through. How can I go back to that place, that house, to what? To carry on slaving away and keeping myself decent? Who for? If I do go back, I'll go on the game. If I go back, that's it, nothing will be the same again, I'm telling you that now. I'll do it tonight.'

'Don't talk nonsense. On Wednesday, I'll talk to Sister María and see if she can help you out in some way, since you have no family.'

'Thanks,' said Mila resentfully, 'but don't bother. I don't need the few scraps of charity they'll give me. If

I go back, I swear on my mother's grave that I'll do what I said I'm going to do.'

Without turning to look at her, Mariano said:

'Fine, you're a grown-up. It's your decision. You'll probably think differently tomorrow. You don't know what you're saying right now.'

Mila sat hunched in her seat and said nothing more. She covered her eyes with her hands, drew her feet up onto the seat, and sat curled like a snail, hugging the warmth of her own body, her hands clutching her knees to her belly. She couldn't stop shivering. The doctor continued to offer advice, but then he gave up talking too. She was aware of him looking at her now and then. Then the car came to a halt and he must have told some child to tell the women, because they arrived at once, talking loudly and excitedly. She, however, waited and refused to budge until they dragged her out. They must have removed the child from the back seat first, judging from the noises she heard. She didn't want to look. Her hands were icy cold.

Mariano stayed where he was, watching the other women half-carrying, half-dragging her down to the hollow where the whitewashed houses were. He waited in case she should turn and look at him, say one last word, but she didn't. There was still time to call out to her. The women formed a whole, of which she was a part, a blurred shape moving down the steps, and the words they said to her and the sound of her sobbing, grown quieter now, gradually moved off. It was night. The clouds had parted to reveal pools of stars. Mariano got back into the car. He wound down the windows. It was nearly ten o'clock. Isabel would be furious with him. He drove along the main street at fifty miles an hour, letting the soft, damp air blow in. He was always late. 'And I bet it was one of those non-paying patients too,' Isabel would say. But he couldn't think about Isabel now. So what if she was angry? He wouldn't phone her tonight. Into his mind came the image of Mila with her face buried in his chest. Take me somewhere. Take me. Take me. He still had time to go back for her. He put his foot down again. Sixty miles an hour. He could take her somewhere for the night. They didn't have to go to his place. Pancho was in America right now, they could use his studio. She'd like it there. He could stay with her. 'I won't be back for supper, Mama.' God, how stupid. He accelerated again. Seventy miles an hour. He passed the entrance to the metro. He was out of the neighbourhood now. He breathed a sigh of relief. He must be mad. He had already gone beyond the call of duty. Way beyond. And he was under no obligation to do anything. Another doctor wouldn't have gone to half as much bother. He must be mad. Why was his conscience still troubling him? If she wanted to go with some man, what did that have to do with him? God knows, it was hardly the first time something like that had happened. She might turn out to be a real weirdo, desperate for a way out of there. Fancy thinking he could take her home! What madness. Especially as it was none of his business anyway. He'd talk to Sister María about her on Wednesday. The car was slipping smoothly along, and Mariano was feeling better. He wouldn't say anything to Isabel about the child having died on the back seat. Given how superstitious she was, she might feel funny about it and not want to ride in the car again. He'd have a shower when he got in, but first, he'd call Isabel. Of course he would. Even if they did have a bit of an argument. Oh, if only they could get married right away.

In Cibeles, he joined the stream of other cars. It was a really beautiful night now.

Madrid, January 1956

Restless Eyes

Medardo Fraile

He could hear only the sound of running water in the bathroom. He was sitting by the window in an old rocking chair, reading the newspaper. Now and then, he gazed vaguely out at the sky and yawned. The soft glow of evening reached as far as the corridor. A light was on in a bedroom in the interior of the apartment. It had been on for more than an hour, a soft, tenuous light, from a bedside lamp. He heard the bathroom door close and, shortly afterwards, the sound of water filling the bath stopped. Now he could hear gentle splashings and tricklings and soapy cascadings. He quickly folded up the newspaper and placed it on his knees. He yawned again and glanced up at a calendar on the wall: Saturday, 5 April.

He closed his eyes and fell instantly asleep. The newspaper slid off his lap and onto the floor.

When the light came on, he opened his eyes.

'I must have fallen asleep,' he murmured, rubbing his face with one hand and stretching slightly.

Then he picked up the newspaper, tossed it onto the table, got to his feet, and lowered the blind; then, drawing the rocking chair closer to the table and the light, he sat down again and began to read the back page.

'So what do you say? Shall we have supper?' she said, leaning in the doorway, her hair caught up on the top of her head, her newly washed body wrapped in a soft, clinging bathrobe.

'Yes, if you like,' he answered, his words distorted by another long yawn.

She came into the room and lowered the blind properly. A few of the slats hadn't quite closed. Then she plugged in the radio, bending her head towards it and looking up, until the distant, burbling thread of a trite little tune and a presenter's voice made themselves heard and immediately filled the whole room. She carefully tamed the voice until it was warm and gentle, like a familiar caress, like the slow, soft touch of bathwater on thighs. The sharp, wild, blithe music of Saturday, the music of the Saturday night variety programmes, brought the apartment back to life.

Now, intermittently, beneath the music, he could hear the clatter of pots and pans in the kitchen, drawers being opened and closed, sometimes the sudden gush of water in the sink or a chair briefly scuffing the floor. And, all the while, the Saturday melody was filling the shadowy corners of the apartment, like a long, silent, surreptitious puff of smoke.

They sat down to eat.

'Do you know, I dozed off.'

'Don't you recognize this music?' she said, looking up at a point above his head. Her face brightened and she smiled slightly:

'It's the music your nephew, Roberto, used to like.'

'What do you mean "*my* nephew"? Isn't he your nephew too?'

'It's nice. Jones Farducci played it on the guitar in that film ... oh, what was it called now?'

'I don't know,' he said, using his fingers to remove a bit of bone from his mouth.

'Yes, you do. That film ... *Six Men Shoot to Kill.* We saw it one Saturday. You never remember anything.'

'That's your job. Anyway, did you have a good bath?'

'Yes, lovely. You could have had one too.'

'Tomorrow.'

'I like this presenter,' she said suddenly. 'He has a jokey, friendly way of speaking. By the way, have you got the tickets?' she asked, looking gratefully at the radio, as if flirting a little with the presenter.

'Yes, of course. Don't worry,' she heard her husband's voice say beside her.

'So what are we going to see?' she said, delicately using her fork to manoeuvre a bit of gristle to the edge of the plate.

'The one you wanted to see ... you know ... oh, what's it called?'

'*The Moon Girls*?'

'That's it. I've no idea what it'll be like.'

'We'll find out,' she said, getting up.

She tidied the kitchen, then went, first, into the dressing room, and then into the bedroom. He returned to the rocking chair and opened the paper again. The waves of music drowned out the faint sounds of things being fastened, the silken rustle of fabric, the slight click of fingernail on button, the secret carnal whisper of an experienced hand smoothing a stocking. He heard, unhurried and sharp, the tap-tap of heels. Then she appeared at the dining-room door.

'Shall we go?'

He got lethargically to his feet and went into the bathroom, where he gave his hair a quick comb and put on his jacket. On the stairs, as they went down, her footsteps sounded like the hoofbeats of a half-broken mare, nervous, on heat. The click-clack of her heels. He followed behind.

A light, scented breeze was ruffling the trees in the little square at the bottom of the street. Across the way, lights were on in almost every window.

'What time is it?'

'It's ... oh, no, my watch has stopped.'

'Trust you! Well, if we do have time, we can pop into Café Oms for a drink. And you can buy some cigarettes. It's on our way.'

'OK.'

Without looking at him, she slipped her arm through his, and they walked the two blocks to the Cine Gladis in silence. The streets were full of a perceptible nervous excitement, and the soft breeze from the acacias gently brushed the skin of passers-by.

'Shall we go in ... except that, first, you need to find out what time it is!'

He asked a man who happened to be passing. It was half past ten. He stopped to put his watch right.

The café was crowded and noisy, heaving with people, and the waiter walked past them again and again with his tray full of drinks. A constant clink of glasses, plates, and spoons came from behind the bar, and from where they were standing, they could catch a strong whiff of coffee.

'Coffee with a dash for me,' he said.

'And a black coffee for me.'

'Do you want anything else to drink?'

'All right. I'll have one if you're having one.'

People were already going into the cinema. The tall, meek, somewhat bored doormen, in their brown uniforms, were allowing in the public in dribs and drabs. The cinema smelled of disinfectant camouflaged by a thick, cloying perfume. 'Icecreamsgetyouricecreamshere!' cried a young lad standing at the front. There was a burst of music, loud at first, then soft and melodic, reaching into every velvety corner, as the people padded across the carpets, talking in slightly hushed tones.

She occasionally spoke to him while they waited, but still without looking at him, without seeing him. She was speaking to a largish shape with the faculty of hearing, but who was an obstacle to her eyes—which looked sometimes to the left and sometimes to the right—an obstacle that always prevented her physically or psychologically from seeing further, seeing other things. She had grown used to talking to him. She barely turned her head when she did so. Her neck remained erect, strong, flexible, and full of pretty little shadows beneath the dark, silky locks of her hair.

'Isn't that the couple who live on the third floor? Yes, it is.'

'It's nice this music, isn't it?'

As the lights went down, he said:

'Well, let's see what *The Moon Girls* have to offer!'

The subject of the film was a group of bored young women, disillusioned with life, who volunteer to fly rockets to the moon. They enter a secret military training base that specializes in space experiments, and where some equally bored and disillusioned young men are being trained for the same purpose. They have to submit to a regime of harsh discipline, but otherwise, they have everything they need and a certain degree of comfort. The young men and women eye each other with about as much interest as if they were viewing a line of telegraph poles. In the bar, they exchange jaundiced views, all the while regarding each other with something approaching distaste and utter indifference. However, the healthy lifestyle and rigid routine, the lack of time to think, triggers in each of them a rebirth of strength, optimism, and an incipient, ever-growing fear that they might die during the experiment. Three couples become romantically attached and get up to all kinds of adventures in their attempts to thwart the commanding officer's ban on them leaving the camp to get married. Their officers, cornered and sweating, finally succumb to the exigencies of love. So filled with regret are they that they promise to give the brides away on their wedding day and to provide them all afterwards with safe posts at the base. The film ends at the door of the church, with everyone happy and smiling beneath a rain of rice. The moon smiles dotingly down on them. Meanwhile, back at the base, a beggar, who has been hanging around the camp, is being signed up as a crew member and, happily chewing on a hunk of stale bread, he strides over to the launch rocket, takes a seat in the cabin, and starts merrily pressing all the buttons, meanwhile beaming at the audience.

They filed slowly out of the cinema.

'It wasn't too bad, I suppose. A bit daft though,' he said, stringing out the words on a long yawn.

She was walking slowly along, not talking. Films made her silent. She was listening to what the people behind them were saying. She paused calmly to wait for a car approaching in the distance to pass. As she walked, she stretched her legs with a kind of grave elegance, assured, measured, supple, suggestive of an attractive, inward-turned, mature indifference. She could hear the murmured conversations of various groups of people as they set off down side streets or parted company with friends. Others were strolling unhurriedly towards the metro. She was filled by a pleasant sensation, by the playful, flickering flame of a vague desire, the savour of a different world, a world of carefree, amusing people, who spouted clever nonsense while gazing lovingly at each other, and whose only thought was to kiss and dance and defeat death at all costs. Of all the characters, she had taken a particular fancy to John, a gawky figure with a child's eyes and cheerful canine teeth!

They reached their street, lit by the cool, silent moon. A cat crossed her path, proud, alert, noiseless. Behind her, in the distance, she heard the lone, echoing footsteps of a man, young, confident, slow, scything a path along the startled pavement. The steps were getting nearer. They sounded closer now. She thought: 'That's how the actor, that cheeky fellow John must walk in real life. I wonder what his name is.'

They reached their building.

'Here we are!'

She went in and, while he was turning the key in the lock, she grasped the grille on the heavy street door, as if waiting for him to finish. The man following behind passed at precisely that moment. He was a dark, stocky young man, who, oblivious to her presence, glanced casually in through the door. She was standing motionless behind the grille, nonchalant, apparently distracted, a glint of boldness and fear in her restless eyes, following the man as he passed, following the wake left behind by his slow, deliberate, swaying walk, by the sound of his sudden rasping cough. She felt the cold iron beneath her hand and saw the closed door. There was Saturday striding off down the street. She realized that her husband was holding the glass-panelled door open for her to pass. And she turned and calmly, silently followed him, one step at a time; and for some reason, she slipped a hand, bewildered and perplexed, into her handbag, as if feeling for something, a key, her powder compact, her handkerchief, that missing piece of Saturday.

Mozart, K. 124,* for Flute and Orchestra

Jorge Ferrer-Vidal

When we used to write to each other in the summer, Carmen, you always used to say in your letters, in every single one of them, as if it were as essential and routine as the date: *you have a little girl's writing, so perfect and precise that it's hard, Jorge, to identify your heart behind it.*

And I seemed to hear your loud, open, heartfelt laughter, because you always laughed from the heart, and then I would remember what you looked like: reddish hair,

---

* K. 124 is actually Mozart's Symphony No. 15 in G. The author presumably meant either K. 313 or K. 314.

slender figure, oval face, blue eyes, and charmingly irregular teeth, and I would long for the holidays to be over, Carmen, so that we could get back to university and rush from class to class, not even hearing what we were told by the temporary lecturers—because we never even saw the professors or the assistant professors. We were the very embodiment of what one teacher of Prehistory used to say: a university lecture consists of a gentleman speaking so loudly that his fifty or so students can hardly hear what they're muttering to each other.

The best part began with those late March afternoons, already longer and slower, with their shy, blush-pink clouds and white nimbus anticipating the arrival of spring. This lasted through April and May until the end of term, with the days growing warmer, even hot.

That, Carmen, was when we would skip our Sociology class, from five to six in the evening, and go and lie on the lawns that covered the area between the Law Faculty and ours, and, seated on that blessed turf, on those lawns newly woken from their winter sleep, we would take out our flutes, you from your bag and I from mine, and play extracts from Mozart's Concerto for Flute and Orchestra, K. 124, but with two flutes and no orchestra. As I pointed out to you once:

'What about the orchestra, Carmen? A concerto should be accompanied by an orchestra. Our dear Wolfgang might disapprove.'

And you, your eyes taking on the blue of the sky itself, responded:

'This is the orchestra,' and you made a sweeping gesture with your hand, 'the orchestra is the evening, the blue sky, the world, you and I, the orchestra is God.'

And it really did seem to us then that the good God was the great orchestrator of our lives, because everything around us oozed happiness, to the point where you would often say, while we were walking hand in hand along Avenida Complutense, that there was something immoral and unjust about our love, and that such selfish happiness shouldn't exist in a world in which hunger, injustice, and utter lovelessness prevailed. I agreed, but, of course, I didn't think about the hungry as I do now, now that I'm lost to you and to myself, and capable only of finding myself and my identity in my fellow men.

Today, Carmen, Wednesday, 16 May 1974, I felt restless at home. It's been a bad, almost sad day, during which I had a long argument with my editor because he insists on setting me these confor st, bourgeois guidelines that I don't understand and tha. I can't apply in my writing, and because the local paper published a rather unfavourable review of my latest novel and, suddenly, I don't know why, I thought of you and wondered what had become of you, and if you had, in the end, married Fernando, and it occurred to me that the only thing that would shake me out of this state of heavy dullness on this unashamedly spring day, like those spring days of ten years ago, would be to return, like Raskolnikov, to the scene of the crime, and so I rummaged around in the drawers for a polo neck sweater and a pair of jeans that I haven't worn in years and which are rather tight, because, Carmen, I've got fatter with the years, and in this disguise, I left my apartment, took the car and here I am, here you have me, thinking of you beneath a pitiliessly unchanged sky still full of clouds, some shyly blushing, others small, white, and sheep-like.

The lawns between the Law Faculty and ours are lush and green, and groups of students, like you and me ten years ago, are lying idly around on the grass, although, when I take a closer look, I notice that there are no couples playing a Mozart duet on flute to the accompaniment of God-the-orchestra.

If you remember, as you must, Carmen, you will agree that, for your sake, I was capable of committing acts of pure folly. That Saturday, you were supposed to be going out with Fernando, and I, in protest, because I couldn't imagine the Faculty without you, came up with an excuse, and the two of us, do you remember, Carmen, went to see Don Ginés Amillo, who had arranged to hold an exam that same day on his subject, Palaeography. You didn't have a clue about Palaeography, being incapable of reading any-thing that wasn't written in as clear and precise a hand as my own girlish writing. Anyway, we tracked down Don Ginés in the department.

'Dr Amillo, both Señorita Romera and I have prior engagements on Saturday and so won't be able to attend the exam.'

And it worked. Don Ginés agreed to let us sit the exam on a Wednesday instead, on 16 May, at four in the afternoon, in the department, fourth floor, room 401, building A, and on that Wednesday, we lunched on sandwiches and beer on the cool, green grass, and then lay down on our backs and played the flute, until the heat of the early afternoon lulled us to sleep, both of us lying there on the lawn, our foreheads touching, but only our foreheads, you understand, because everything between us was limpid and translucent—and orchestrated by God.

Here I am again, Carmen, looking at the same grassy area, the same lawn, and through the open window of my car, parked outside the Faculty, next to the Law Faculty, I can see the large, wide-open windows of room 401 in the Palaeography Department, and I wonder if Don Ginés is invigilating another couple like you and me, although I doubt it. No, there has never been anyone like you and me. Because, if you remember, Carmen, no one will ever do again what I did for you in the few seconds that it took Don Ginés, on that hot day, to leave the room and ask the porter to bring him a cool drink from the bar. I did it because I was even in love with your weak will and because I was convinced that, otherwise, you would fail your degree, because for you, reading Carolingian minuscule in Latin or courtly and legal hands in old Castilian was simply an insuperable obstacle, an impossible goal to achieve with your scant historical vocation and your almost non-existent Latin.

True, the exam was not without its difficulties and problems, in that the scribe who bodged the fourteenth-century original must have been an out-and-out bastard, a terrible fellow, yes, but it wasn't so hard that you couldn't transcribe or decipher a single word, Carmen. Disaster area that you were, a complete lost cause, you couldn't even manage the formulaic introductory sentence, common to all manuscripts of the time and of previous ages too, and which could be found in Carolingian documents and diplomas: *In nomine Domini nostri Iesu Christi, amen. Ego Aedefonsus, rex Castiella, Legionis, Gallecia* ... You couldn't even manage that, Carmen.

And when Don Ginés left the room, saying: 'I'm just going to ask the porter to bring me up a drink. It's terribly hot. Would you like anything?', we shook our heads:

'No, thank you, Don Ginés.'

And he said:

'Now I'm trusting you not to exchange a single word while I'm out of the room.'

We obeyed. We didn't exchange a single word, but we did exchange exam scripts, and you were left with my complete transcription and I with yours, that is, with a blank sheet of paper and with no time in which to transcribe more than half a dozen words of the original because Don Ginés returned a few minutes later and said:

'Time's up. Sign your papers.'

And we duly signed. I'm not reproaching you with anything, certainly not now, ten years on, can you imagine, Carmen, how could I possibly say anything, when it was on my initiative, taking advantage of my own girlish hand, so perfect and precise that Don Ginés took the bait—who wouldn't have?—and so you passed your degree, Carmen, right there and then, while I had to wait for the resits in September.

What I do reproach you with is that you accepted my help as something perfectly natural and inevitable, and didn't even bother to thank me properly, apart from commenting laconically as we left the room:

'Thank you. Now I'll be able to enjoy the summer on the Costa Brava without having to study a word, imagine that, Jorge, the first summer in my entire life when I won't have to study.'

My heart stopped when I learned through Amalia, your best friend, that Fernando was also spending the summer in Tossa de Mar.

What had begun three terms before with our flute concertos, ended there, on Wednesday, 16 May 1964, exactly ten years ago to the day, when we sat that Palaeography exam, and since then, Carmen, I have neither seen you nor heard from you. I don't know if you're alive or dead, if you're married or where you live, and I feel suddenly so upset, sitting here in my car, that I don't even dare drive back home, in case I have an accident, and so I get out of my white Austin 1300 Countryman, with its Soria number plate, SO-13467, and I walk across the lush green grass, sit down under a tree, lean my back against the trunk, take my flute from the back pocket of my too-tight jeans, straining at the seams, and play the first bars of K. 124, for Flute and Orchestra, and when they hear me, a couple lying amorously on the grass look up and smile at me, and she has reddish hair, a slender figure, an oval face, blue eyes, and charmingly irregular teeth.

And I continue playing in the hope that somewhere in the world, wherever that might be, however far away, another flute will join me in the next few bars, and that the long, slow afternoon, swooning from an excess of calm and languor, with rosy nimbus and stratus clouds in the west like giant poppies, will be the orchestral accompaniment to my flute solo. However hard I try, though, I cannot hear your flute beside me, nor does God-the-orchestra respond to my call. 'Carmen,' I wonder, 'what can have become of you? Why does God not answer?'

Through the Wall

Marina Mayoral

You could hear them clearly from the bathroom. And from the bedroom too, although not so well, only in bursts, the occasional word, then nothing. From the bathroom, though, you could hear everything: the splashing, the soap landing, plop, in the water, and the laughter, because initially, I would often hear them laugh. 'Can I come in, Mama?' the child would say; he often called his mother 'Mama' or 'Mammy' and she called him 'poppet' and 'sweetheart'. But the mother seemed somewhat anxious: 'Be careful now... you shouldn't try to get up on your own... that's it, put your dressing gown on, that's better,' she would say. And this is what made me think the child must be ill. I said to Chema, 'We've got new neighbours,' but he wasn't interested. Now he's saying I've started with my obsessions again and doesn't remember me telling him I could hear them in the bathroom and how the little boy would ask his mother to stay with him while he bathed and say to her: 'You're so pretty, Mammy.'

He was only a little boy, but very bright. They obviously weren't Spanish or at least the mother wasn't, she had some kind of Latin American accent, but which part of Latin America I couldn't say—they all sound the same to me—but she had a very soft voice, as did the little boy. 'Will you always stay with me?' he would ask, and his mother would tell him 'Yes', and the little boy would ask: 'And you don't have to go to work any more?' and his mother would tell him 'No', she didn't have to work any more because *'le habían "pegado" la lotería'*—that's what she said—that they had won the lottery, but 'pegado' isn't what we'd say in Spain, and that she would always be with him. I don't know why, but I never believed this, I thought she was just saying it, and that the real reason she didn't work was because the child was ill. And then another night, from the bedroom, I heard him say: 'Mammy, I don't want to go to Heaven, I want to stay here with you.' 'Who's been filling your head with such nonsense? Carmela? The priest? You're not going anywhere, you hear, you'll always stay with Mama, always, poppet.' 'And what will Heaven be like, Mammy?' 'Well, Heaven is a lovely place where you can do all the things you most like doing, but there's no need to think about that now.' And then the little boy said: 'I don't want to leave you alone, Mammy... I'm going to grow up and earn lots of money so that we can go to the beach together.'

They often talked about the beach: 'Tell me again what it's like, Mama,' and his mother would describe a beach with palm trees and warm water and lovely big waves, so big they could overturn boats, and red shells you could hold to your ear and hear the sea, and coral... 'When will we go there, Mammy? ' and she would always say: 'As soon as you're properly better, then we'll go.'

Then, one night, I heard him crying. I couldn't hear what they were saying, only the song she was singing:

> *A la nanita nana, nanita ea,*
> *mi niño tiene sueño, bendito sea,*
> *Pimpollo de canela, lirio en capullo,*
> *duérmete, vida mía, mientras te arrullo...* *

She often sang this to him. It's a very sad song, telling the child to close his eyes and sleep, even if his mother dies without ever again seeing herself reflected in his eyes. She sang another song too:

---

* Lullaby, lullaby, la/my baby is sleepy, bless him/cinnamon shoot, lily in bud/go to sleep, my love, while I sing you to sleep...

El sultán tenía una caña
de oro y plata, á – á – á
con cincuenta ilustraciones
*de hoja de lata, á – á – á.**

When I heard that song, I burst into tears, it's one my father used to sing to me as well. In fact, he used to sing it to me until I was quite old. He would come into my bedroom, while my mother ranted on about how he spoiled me, and he would take his pipe out of his mouth and use it to keep time: '*El sultán* | *tenía una caña* | *de oro y plata* | *á – á – á* ', and I would bury my face in the pillow so that my mother wouldn't hear me laughing and tell us off.

Chema got really annoyed. He sat up in bed, furious: 'What the hell's wrong now?' I woke him up because he wouldn't believe me: 'You're going back to your old ways. You know what the doctor said,' and I told him that this was different. Before, I used to hear a child crying in my sleep and it was the anxiety of hearing the crying that woke me up, but then I would lie there with my eyes open and wouldn't hear a thing. This was different, though, the little boy was there, in the next apartment, I could hear him talking, him and his mother. You could tell by his

---

* The sultan has a cane/of gold and silver, ah – ah – ah/ with fifty illustrations/ made of tin-plate, ah – ah – ah.

voice that he was only small, but so mature, so thoughtful, someone you could talk to. He seemed such a sweet boy and incredibly considerate for a child his age: 'I don't want you to buy me the panda, Mammy, I just wanted to point it out to you, because pandas are so pretty, and you've never seen one, not like me, I saw them for real at the zoo, when Délia took me, she's so nice Délia, when's she coming to visit again? Anyway, don't spend any money, Mammy, I just wanted you to have a look at it, the shop's right next to the market, in a big toy shop.' Chema was never home when they were talking in the bathroom, but often at night, the boy would whimper and cry, and I'd wake Chema: 'Listen, listen now,' I would say, 'he's crying.' Chema would really hit the roof then. 'Hundreds of children cry in Madrid at night. Will you let me sleep? Some of us have to work, you know!'

I told my mother about it. I sometimes go and see her at the boutique. Not often, it's true, why would I? She always tells me off or says nasty things about Chema or Papa: 'If you want to stick your head in the sand, fine, in that respect you're just like your father, but don't come complaining to me about it, just put up with it. He's taking advantage of your money and our family contacts. He's deceiving you, as you well know, and he treats you like dirt, but I'd prefer not to hear about it.' I didn't want to talk to her about Chema, but about the child crying, but it's always the same, we end up talking about whatever she wants to talk about, and she doesn't even listen to me: 'A child? But who are they? Is there no father?'

The doctor took the same approach: 'A woman on her own, a single mother, of course, more or less your age, is that right? And the child is more or less the age yours would be now?' Yes, it's true, but I wanted to explain that it wasn't what he thought, the child really existed, had his own personality, his own way of being—'I don't want to leave you alone, Mammy, I'm going to grow up and earn a lot of money and then we can go to the beach'... 'I don't want you to buy it, Mammy, I just wanted you to see it, pandas are so lovely'—He was obviously from around here, since he knew the toy shop next to the market. True, I'd never seen them and no one knew them, but I could hear them, him and his mother; they were new to the area, that's all, and everyone's always in too much of a hurry to notice anyone else.

I asked the porter in the apartment building next door: 'A young woman and a little boy, she's from Latin America, I think.' I made a quick calculation, they probably lived on the seventh or eighth floor. 'On the right or the left? There are four apartments on each side,' he told me. He was looking at me curiously. 'I live next door. I can hear them at night.' 'Oh, you hear everything in these buildings,' he said, as if he were beginning to understand,

'it's full of students and short-term tenants. It bothers you,
I suppose.' 'Yes,' I said, well, what else could I say, I felt
ashamed to be there, asking after a complete stranger and
clutching a package. It was the panda. I left it in the back
room, so that Chema wouldn't see it. I don't want him to
send me back to the doctor again, they always come out
with the same things: 'There are no physiological reasons
why you can't conceive, you just have to relax, have faith,'
'It's a self-punishing process which has its basis in guilt
feelings and an unnaturally strong bond with your father,'
'You're getting obsessed again, Cristina, please, call the
analyst, he'll explain it to you, and let me rest, I have to
work, you know. I'm exhausted,' 'You've always stuck your
head in the sand, just like your father...come on now,
Cris, when was the last time? You can't fool me, dissatis-
faction shows. Look, I know you, you're a strong, healthy
girl, and it all went perfectly well in London, they know
what they're doing there, they take things like that in their
stride, so don't worry, it's not your fault...If you can't get
pregnant it's because of him, he knows what he's doing, he
always has...'

I know it was wrong. I should have told my mother
I wanted to have the baby and marry Chema, but instead
I went to London with her and we waited for Chema to
finish his degree. 'Finish his degree? Let's not beat about
the bush, dear, he waited until you were twenty-one and

could inherit your father's money.' I know it was wrong, and it's true what the psychiatrist says, I do feel guilty, but not that guilty. I know Papa would forgive me, he was so kind and understanding. The doctor was a kind man too, he was getting on a bit, but his own father was still alive; they chose the same profession, and he really admired his father, and so he understood me better than the psychiatrist, and since there were no physiological reasons or mental ones, the thing is...I just blurted it out and I think I blushed. He patted me on the shoulder and smiled fondly: 'Forget about the child and his mother. Forget about your husband too, come to that. Have fun, try and enjoy yourself!'

It was foolish of me to buy the panda, because no one in the neighbourhood knew the mother or the child. I asked the greengrocer and the baker: 'They must live in one of those apartments,' they said, and they didn't know Carmela either, although, of course, she didn't come very often. 'Is she a tall, well-built woman?' they asked, but, of course, I didn't know what she looked like, or the mother or the boy. It occurred to me that perhaps the mother might want to buy the panda, so I took it back to the shop and asked them for a voucher, said I'd come back another day, and they put it in the shop window again, where it stayed. I could still hear the voices, though. Not so much in the bathroom, I didn't hear them laughing together there, they were always in the bedroom. She would read him stories and they must have played Monopoly sometimes as well, because I heard him say: 'I'll buy two houses and a hotel. ' I used to play Monopoly with Papa, and after I saw the little sister of a friend of mine, all stiff and purple, I became terrified of dying too. Papa was furious with my mother for taking me to see her. He very rarely got angry, but that day, he did. And he always said to me: 'You mustn't think of sad, ugly things, you must think that it's like a dream and that when you wake up, I'll be there waiting for you, singing and keeping time with my pipe: *"el sultán | tenía una caña | de oro y plata | á – á – á "*.' That's more or less what the boy's mother had said: 'You're not going to Heaven, poppet, I'll go everywhere with you, like this, hand in hand, you see, I won't let you go alone, we'll always be together. ' Then, for several days, I heard nothing, apart from one morning, the noise of cleaning, and then from the bathroom, I heard: 'I look so ugly with no hair!' And she: 'It'll soon grow again, you'll see, and it'll be thicker and fairer than ever.' 'Mammy, I'm not sure we'll be able to go to the beach.' 'Of course we will, you've just got to fatten up a bit so that the waves won't carry you off. I couldn't take you there now when you're so thin.' And that night: 'Mammy, Mama, give me your hand.' That was the last thing I heard him say, then I heard more women's voices and someone crying as well, yes, it seemed to me that someone was sobbing, but perhaps that wasn't them, perhaps that was coming from another apartment.

I haven't asked about them again, there's no point, it's obvious that no one knew them, that they were new to the area, just passing through. She didn't do the shopping, she must have had a home help to do that, and the little boy didn't go out to play because he was ill. He must have recovered enough for them to go off to that beach of big waves and warm water. He'll get fatter there and grow up big and strong just as he said he would. He was such a responsible, intelligent child, she'll never be alone with a son like that, even if she does have to work, even if she doesn't have much money. She never did buy that panda, but perhaps she was saving up her money to go to that marvellous beach. He was a very serious boy for his age, because you could tell from his voice that he was only young, and from what she said, he must have been quite small too ... Yes, that's what must have happened: he got better and they've gone away.

Return Journey

Carlos Castán

I noticed her shortly after the train had set off; she was sitting with her head resting against the speeding land-scape. My first impulse was to open my newspaper and hide behind all the news that I would not now be reading, news so remote it seemed to belong to another world, news that was suddenly utterly irrelevant. It was Marta.

And with her, with that face and those gestures I thought long forgotten, with that old familiar sadness, a whole era swam into my mind, possibly a golden era. But whenever I recall those days, when life and long hours at school still lay before us, the days of Marta and sitting in cafés after classes, of books to read and Saturdays from which one disembarked with a knife between one's teeth, whenever I return to that time, I always find, beneath the sweet surface of rumbustious youth, the pain of open wounds still unhealed and, with the passing of the years, transformed into shadows where my memory prefers not to linger, but from which it absorbs, as it skims by, the disquiet they exude, the confused echo of their moans. Sometimes memories are like noises on the stairs.

Hidden behind my newspaper, eavesdropping on her occasional remarks to the older woman and the children travelling with her, I evoked the faces of friends whose names I thought I no longer knew, the inhabitants of a time when we were just waking up to an astonishing world, exciting and cruel, that was already urgently tugging at us; and I remembered the shabby classrooms, the smell of the overheated projector on which, during the final period on Monday afternoons, they used to show us art slides, while out in the street, in winter, the first street lamps and neon signs were lighting up, and roaring past beneath the windows were the buses, laden with stories, heading for the centre, the brightly lit buses we almost never took, but which were there, like a hope, like a promise, and which, in exchange for a few coins, would carry us across the frontiers of the known world, far from the narrow stage of our lives.

The first time I saw Marta, I watched her for ages, for about five or six hours, without once taking my eyes off her. It was my first day at a new secondary school, and

I arrived filled with the sense of alarm and dread that everyone feels on arriving in some noisy, unfamiliar place. She knew nearly everyone already and was laughing and greeting people to right and left; while I, at the other end of the classroom, gazed at her mane of blonde hair, her angel eyes, her mouth in continual motion, either because she was speaking or because of the strawberry-flavoured gum she was constantly chewing. Then she sat down at a desk next to one of the radiators and took out her little girl's pencil case and a file plastered with photos of James Dean. From there, she scanned the whole room again and again, apparently looking for something, as if before the noonday bell rang, she had to have chosen her fate, her next adventure, a soul she could wound. The challenge for me, despite my blushes and my churning blood, was to hold her gaze, to make her look away first or turn her head.

When school finished, I usually headed off down Calle Puerto Rico towards Avenida de Concha Espina to get the number 43 bus. One day, Marta caught up with me; as usual, she was accompanied by her younger sister, who was a year or two below us, a girl whose shyness and large round glasses belied a certain prettiness, and who was, for the most part, Marta's hesitant apprentice, a silent, smiling witness to her sister's restless exuberance, Marta going hither and thither, first with this person, then with that, flitting from flower to flower, now roaring with laughter, now telling a joke, now blowing a kiss, now tossing her long mane of fair hair. Marta came up to me and said something about how I always seemed so alone and somehow sad, and we talked about this and that, the usual thing, until they turned off to go home. For many days afterwards, I took the same route, casting occasional backward glances, hoping they would catch me up, walking as slowly as possible, lingering outside every shop window, but, as far as I remember, the encounter was never repeated, or else Marta and her sister were with a lot of other people, or stopped to join another group of students, or, at the last moment, crossed over to the other side.

I can, if I try, still feel that sense of loneliness, the loneliness of walking slowly along, thinking that, at any moment, I might hear her voice behind me and her own very particular silence, the silence that occurred in between the shouting, the laughter, and the roar of car engines. And I felt all that again in the train, hunched in my seat, still alone and somewhat sad; I felt it so intensely that I simply had to get up and go over to her, the woman who had Marta's same eyes and skin, and who was, at that moment, taking a couple of fruit yoghurts out of a bag to give to her children, and who immediately remembered my name and stood up, happy and confused, and introduced me to her mother-in-law and, almost in the same breath, announced that she was going to the buffet bar with this new-found old friend, who had just resurfaced after years and years.

We sat down at one of the tables in the buffet car and started talking about those long-lost years, about how we had imagined our lives would be and how they had actually turned out, and we wondered what had become of the classmates who had once been our inseparable friends and whom we hadn't seen since. She provided me with a few snippets of fairly recent information about some of her girlfriends from schooldays, whose names rang distant bells, but for whom my memory, in most cases, had not preserved a face. I told her that I'd bumped into Urzaiz, the anarchist rebel who had dreamed of setting fire to the school office, and who was now a broken, balding man in suit and tie, working nine hours a day as section head in a finance company. We talked about a thousand other things, about our schooldays and about now, about how everything turns sour, about children, about the concerts we used to go to at the university halls of residence, and we sang the old familiar song that asks where all those shared, heartfelt dreams have gone, the same way as the little money we had at the time and the bottle we used to pass from hand to hand as we sat on the grass.

But while she evoked vague memories of a lost and splendid age, I recalled things of which she seemed to know nothing, although she kept nodding and smiling. For example, the moment, exactly a year after that first meeting, when we became an item, or, rather, comrades wearing identical green fatigues, just like Che's, bought in the Rastro one rainy Sunday, comrades shoulder to shoulder in the street and with the revolution still before us, she with her long hair waving in the breeze and me clutching dog-eared copies of Benedetti novels; well, it was never just the two of us, of course, we were always surrounded by people, with no time for love, with so much to do, meetings to organize, the layout for the magazine to prepare, and more meetings. Besides, she assiduously avoided being alone with me, because she couldn't make up her mind, because she was afraid and didn't fancy camping out in the mountains or staying in some seedy hotel in the centre, the kind where prostitutes haunt the stairs, which was all we could have afforded, or of spending our first night together accompanied by the coughs of ageing syphilitics. Besides, there was so much else to do, there was the theatre group, there was fear—no, I can't make this Saturday—and more fear—I've got my period—and there was my bourgeois dream of walking hand in hand with her beside the sea, beneath a starry sky.

She summoned up stories about our teachers and the caretakers, who seemed old enough to be our ancestors as they shuffled down the corridors. But she appeared to have forgotten the afternoon when she and I, unaided, removed all the crucifixes and the framed reproductions of Franco's testament from every classroom on the second floor and dumped them in the rubbish bins. When we were asked who was to blame for this outrage, I stepped forward and was duly suspended for three days, whereas she said nothing because her father would have killed her if he found out, and so we were never, as I hoped we would be, two commie outcasts, walking, arms about each other, through the school grounds, exchanging kisses and simultaneously pricking the consciences of our classmates inside, who were busily filling their exercise books with maths problems.

While we reminisced about our group outings to the old Cinestudio Griffith, those evenings of Bogart and *Novecento*, of *Johnny Got His Gun* and *Jonas qui aura 25 ans en l'an 2000*, and the beers we drank in bars on the way home, I became lost in vain speculations about the capricious nature of the individual memory, which, when it takes us back, when it turns its eyes on a time and place of shared experiences, leads us into radically different worlds, contradictory events and unrecognizable cities adrift in varicoloured fogs, pink mists and grey mists that suddenly leave your heart homeless, mists as black as the darkest night. So whereas, for some, the realm of the past is pure perfumed nostalgia, a flowery path through a leafy, shady grove, for others, removing the lid from the box of memories resembles that moment in horror films when the graves open and ghosts emerge ready for war, corpses on horseback, who leave behind in the night a trail of howls and tattered black shrouds.

We ordered another two brandies and continued mulling over the old days. She seemed not to know what I meant when I spoke of the slight air of bitterness that used to surround me then, always so alone, always somehow sad, as you yourselves used to say, surrounded by people, but on another planet, a cold planet too far away to hear the echo of your laughter and the music that got you all up on the floor dancing. She spoke of the euphoric sense we had then that we could change everything, a feeling not found in the youth of today, not at all, a desire for freedom that flowed in our blood and made us in its own image and that still moves us and sometimes kicks inside us like a fiery horse, it's an ache from the past, and that ache is unrelenting, my friend, an insistent pulse that imposes a kind of dignity on us. But she said nothing of the hell I suffered then and still do even now in nightmares, and I preferred not to mention it to her either, although it returns like a chasm along which I feel my way like a blind man with a stick, no, not a yawning precipice, but pure pain, nothing more, the pain that's there when you turn on the light, when you get dressed ready to face another day, because you carry it inside you. It's an intimate part of the way you see things, it's the damp in your bones, and the weight of the days through which you're forced to trudge. She said nothing about Pradillo—the working-class heart-throb, with his suede bomber jacket and his slicked-back hair, with his gold Real Madrid key ring and his absurd hard-man persona, like some nightclub bouncer, who embodied everything we hated—about how he got locked in the toilet and started screaming hysterically, suddenly overwhelmed by feelings of claustrophobia, so much so that, in the end, they had to send for the locksmith; about how half the school were there, watching the man working away and listening to Pradillo's screams; and how, when the locksmith finally opened the door, Marta was there too, sitting on the lavatory seat, her hands covering her face. She wouldn't speak to anyone, certainly not to me. She abandoned the theatre group and happiness and the magazine and me and everything, and was never again the same frolicsome Marta, who was always here, there, and everywhere; instead, she remained as alone and silent as when she walked out of the toilets past the suppressed giggles and murmurs. After that, she was never seen without Pradillo, who seemed more like her bodyguard than anything more enviable, and she never relinquished that deeply entrenched silence, which, as far as I was concerned, had lasted until that afternoon on the train.

When we returned to our seats, her children and her mother-in-law were all deep asleep. There was almost another hour to go before we arrived, and we had drunk too much brandy to be able to settle down and read. It was one of those moments when you can almost hear the soundtrack of a film in which you have suddenly, without realizing, become one of the protagonists. There we were, the two of us, a tipsy glint in our eyes, unable to read or do anything apart from gaze at each other, she smiling now and then, smoothing her skirt and then again looking up at me. I got to my feet and suggested one last drink or perhaps a strong coffee to clear our heads a bit, and so we headed back to the buffet. This time, I held her hand. However, on the way to the buffet, we had no time to think about that, because what with our already slightly unsteady state and the swaying of the train, we stumbled in one of those spaces between carriages, where the doors are and the fire extinguisher and the heating controls, and in order not to fall, we grabbed hold of each other, and stood for a moment poised, as if about to launch into a dance, like a couple in a perfume ad; and after a brief interrogatory glance that our mildly inebriated state made still briefer, I felt her tongue in my mouth like a slow, warm fish telling me to take what was mine, to seize what I had left behind and that had been lost for far too long, but which was there now for the taking, in its proper place. When no one was looking, we shut ourselves in one of the toilets, where I could finally run my fingers through her hair and make love to her against the metal sink, where a metallic breeze blew in up the plughole. Where I could experience, after all those years, the kind of love I deserved and had never enjoyed, a mixture of tenderness and wild abandon, blood and roses, and I lost myself in that unexpected sweetness, like a child in the night, and not for one second did I consider rejecting a single drop of the distant pain brought to me by that long-postponed pleasure (the pain of not being able to hold on to the moment, of having trudged through thousands of days like some monotonous steamroller, the pain of Pradillo, of every bus not taken because we were too afraid, the pain of arriving late at a place where the person waiting had long since gone), that made me feel both the wound and the pleasure of revenge.

Chill reality greeted us when we said goodbye on the platform, surrounded by children and suitcases—winter again; I wanted to look deep into her eyes and pronounce a grave 'Goodbye, Marta', putting real feeling into every syllable, so that my words would remain for ever seared on her memory like one of those unmissable moments in anyone's album of life, whose pages would flash rapidly before her eyes if ever she was in an accident and her car turned over. She didn't seem in the least put out when she replied, laughing, that she wasn't Marta, but Begoñita, her sister, the one with the glasses, with a tendency to acne, the one who was so often left at home watching TV with her parents when I went to call for Marta, the one who had never made anyone's heart skip a beat, the one who, from her second row seat, had been the silent observer of other people's lives. And then I realized that in that grubby train toilet rattling its way towards winter, there had been more than one act of revenge and more than one person's pain among the torn buttons, sweat, moans, and smeared lipstick.

Flying Fish

Eloy Tizón

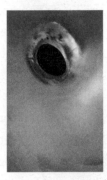

At home, we always had a fish bowl containing two or three goldfish; it wasn't anything very special, but it added to the atmosphere; in my family, we always had a soft spot for the modest, greyish, somewhat worse-for-wear fish at the back of the shop window, at least that's what we told everyone, and we had the fish at home to prove it. Sometimes a suspicious thread would be seen emerging from their bellies, like an endless yellow tape measure, and that was the sign that the water in the bowl needed changing. On some mornings, before my sisters and I went off to school, we would notice that a fish was missing—where's the fish, what fish, which fish do you think, the fat one with the greenish scales—and when my father came home that evening from work, he would gather us all together in

204 ■ Eloy Tizón

the living room and explain kindly that when he got up that morning, he had noticed that the fish was looking rather sad and glum, in a word, unwell, and that he had thrown it into the Manzanares river on his way to the office so that the fish might revive.

We didn't know whether to believe him or not. My sisters and I found the story distinctly odd, but for my part, I preferred, as a matter of course, not to dig too deeply but to let matters lie. I never liked asking questions, and I still don't. There was something creepy about the idea of our father catching the early train to the office, with the sad fish stuffed in his jacket pocket or God knows where, and the other passengers watching our father get up, walk determinedly out into the corridor, struggle to open the window just enough to reveal a crack of cold and dark and snow, and then remove from his pocket or his briefcase the plump, sad, wriggling fish and throw it from the bridge into the windy waters of the Manzanares.

No, we weren't sure whether to believe him. The fish's acrobatic fate seemed frankly incredible, and it was hard to reconcile the image of our very proper and efficient father sitting in his office with the image of him engaging in such a furtive, humiliating, undignified activity. On the mornings when he had to throw a fish into the river, it upset us somehow to think of our father, later on, in the office, amidst the hurly-burly of work, busy as a goldsmith at his desk, with his pipe and his balance sheets, with his usual outdoorsy smell, all part of making that little extra effort to keep the household going. For no reason I can put my finger on, he seemed to us more alone then, fishless and riverless, slaving away in his shirtsleeves, and we tended to think of him as being more vulnerable on those days when he had to throw the fish in the river.

I don't know how many fish flew into that river, but there must have been at least a dozen, and by the following evening, without fail, as if by magic, a new individual would have appeared in the fish bowl—look at his fins and his beautiful gills, the fish was almost transparent against the soapy light and floated like music around the convex walls, let's see how long this one lasts.

That's how it was, one fish took the place of another, and a long chain of ill-fated experiments linked the first to the last. Over a period of months, a whole melancholy collection of strange, sickly creatures ended up in the feeble current of the Manzanares. We're single-handedly repopulating the ocean, my father would say and then laugh that laugh of his that was neither happy nor sad.

Seeing him set off bright and early with the defective fish only to return when it was dark with the new fish in his briefcase were the two halves of a single movement. To my sisters and myself, it seemed that the search for and inspection of fish were part of a father's responsibilities.

They're weak, have no resistance, a slight change in the temperature is enough for even the most prudent of fish to catch a cold and spend hours lethargically opening and closing its mouth as if calling for help. It's a depressing sight, there's nothing more heartbreaking than living in the same apartment as a doomed fish.

How my father must have hated those crisp, cold winter mornings, the dark apartment, the freezing kitchen, when he had no option but to be a good father and plunge his hand into the water and grope around until he found the slippery, viscous silhouette—my father's fingers in the fish bowl, the slow, warm shadow of the artificial waterweed brushing his knuckles—and how he must have hated the sheer irrationality of then having to go on being a father all day and every day, without respite, grappling with work, waterweed, and gills.

Grey. The waters of the Manzanares are grey. And at dawn, in the months of January and February, a pale dampness, like a frosty incense, rises from its banks. The waters of the river are murky and the train windows hard to open, in fact, you're not supposed to open them at all, and our father had to do all that, and break the law, simply to keep faith with his family and restore health to the fish and the fish to the river, like a fisherman in reverse.

One day, I decided to give him a helping hand. I got up even earlier than you, Papa, and placed your briefcase in readiness next to your overcoat—are you listening, Papa—I was practically asleep on my feet, but so full of love for you, and then to pass the time, I went to the toilet.

Just as I was about to pull the chain, I got a real fright: there, bobbing about at the bottom of the bowl lay the latest sickly fish, now deceased and wearing a sinister grin. In a second, the mystery of the Manzanares was solved. I decided to say nothing, the cataract swept the unfortunate corpse down into the muddy labyrinth of sewers and drains, at the end of which it would perhaps emerge into some fragrant fishing ground. The moment I saw the fish's dead body, I bade farewell to my childhood self, to that small boy peering into the toilet bowl.

That night, our father came home in a particularly good mood, smelling, as usual, of the outdoors, and bringing with him an incredible pair of fish, fresh from the tropics—now don't be silly, come and see them, aren't they beautiful. But I wanted nothing more to do with them, I couldn't stand the sight of fish, they grated on my nerves, and whenever Christmas or my birthday approached, and I was asked what kind of pet I would like as a present, I would say thank you, but I'd much rather have a pen.

Let the Passengers Out

José Ferrer-Bermejo

To his surprise he finds himself back on the platform, now empty of people again, and sits down on one of the benches. He tries to stay calm and think it through; he carefully lights a cigarette and takes a deep breath of warm subway air. He stares at the big advertising hoardings on the opposite platform: a make of shoe, an airline, a soft drink. He also notices the vending machines selling bars of chocolate and chewing gum, the benches, the litter bins... In the little glass-fronted office a sleepy attendant is sitting at a table leafing through a newspaper. It's obvious: there's just been a slip-up, a series of stupid mistakes, it could happen to anyone. Drawing deeply on his cigarette, he reconstructs events: he got on the metro at Argüelles at around half past six; after he left work, he had spent some time buying cotton handkerchiefs in the department store on the corner of Calle Princesa and Calle Alberto Aguilera, and then had to hurry to keep an appointment; he went down to the platform for the trains to Sol, the train arrived as usual and passed in succession the various stations, exactly as expected: Ventura Rodríguez, Plaza de España, Callao, Sol. He had calmly got out when the doors opened, taking care, as always, not to get his foot caught in the gap between train and platform; he then took the corridor leading to the Calle Mayor exit and he distinctly remembers dropping a coin onto the handkerchief spread out by a young man who was sitting on the floor playing a guitar; a few steps beyond the busker, a Gypsy woman with a baby sleeping in her arms was holding out her hand to beg for a coin, which he, as usual, tendered politely and with pleasure, and then, after turning a couple of corners and going up and down a few flights of stairs, he found himself back on the same platform he had just left. On the opposite platform, a woman wearing glasses and standing by the advertisement for shoes stared at him insistently, and feeling suddenly ridiculous, he hastily turned to look at the plan of the metro on the wall behind him, to conceal the embarrassed rush of blood to his face. He recovered quickly, however—after all, anybody can make a mistake, and he was in a hurry, a big hurry, to keep his appointment; so he went back to the corridor leading to the Calle Mayor exit, past the Gypsy woman who was still begging; he turned a corner, went down some stairs, up some other stairs ... And felt a shiver when he saw the same advertisements for a make of shoe, the airline, the soft drink, the same benches, the same vending machines selling chewing gum and bars of chocolate, the same attendant reading the newspaper in his office, the same woman wearing glasses, who was now staring at him with growing curiosity.

It's that sudden cold shiver that has made him sit down on one of the benches, light a cigarette, and examine the situation carefully. There are days when your brain isn't in gear, when things like this do happen, especially if you add in a few problems, a lot of things to think about, and above all a very important appointment, one that has been occupying his thoughts for a long time now. His haste and maybe also his nerves have played a nasty trick on him, and now, as the platform begins to fill up again with passengers, he can see the funny side. It's obvious what has happened: nothing to get worked up about, anyone can make a mistake, even if they've spent a lifetime travelling on the metro.

Suddenly he notices a distant hum, which gradually gets nearer and nearer, until a train rushes in from his left, stopping on the opposite tracks with a strange squeal of brakes; the doors open and after a few seconds there's a whistling sound and off it goes towards Moncloa. The woman with the glasses carries on staring at him from a carriage window until the train disappears into the blackness of the tunnel. Then another train emerges from his right and he stares, without really seeing it, at the message above each door: LET THE PASSENGERS OUT. He finishes his cigarette and with a sigh thinks to himself that this whole thing has just been absolutely stupid.

But now he has to hurry, he can't hang around any longer if he's to arrive on time for his appointment. He picks up his packet of cotton handkerchiefs and ventures once more down the corridor leading to the Calle Mayor exit; he smiles with satisfaction when he hears the young guitarist still playing and then the mumbled phrases of the Gypsy begging for money; he turns a few corners, passing people hurrying in the other direction, goes down some stairs, up some other stairs, and emerges again on the same platform, with the shoes, the planes, the benches, and the attendant like a statue, reading his newspaper.

He's not smiling any more.

He feels a strange anger inside; he grinds his teeth, and feels like banging his head against the wall. This is stupid, maddening, especially now that he's in a hurry, a big hurry, more and more of a hurry. He paces up and down the platform like a caged lion, cursing under his breath, heedless of the people looking at him out of the corner of their eye (they can go to hell!); he throws his packet of handkerchiefs into a litter bin (he feels now it's the stupidest packet in the universe) and rejects with utter fury all the possible solutions his rational instinct for self-preservation can come up with: Follow somebody? Sure! Everybody's going somewhere, but nobody is going where he has to go, to keep his very important appointment, now endangered by an idiotic mistake that no longer strikes him as the least bit funny. Ask somebody, some attendant? Great idea! So they can take him for a fool, or some illiterate peasant—wasn't it clear enough, the blue letters on a white background saying 'Exit Calle Mayor'? Ask somebody, when he's spent his entire life, ever since he was a child, travelling on the metro? Ask somebody, when he knows by heart all the lines and the names of all the stations? Forget it! He's going out into the street this minute, there's the Puerta del Sol exit, just behind the newspaper kiosk, and when he gets up there he'll see on his left the Security Police headquarters and opposite him Calle Mayor, and a bit further on the café where the person he has arranged to meet will be waiting with growing impatience, and where he intends to order himself a good strong drink to forget this whole terrible business, which has been going on now for far too long: the blame lies with the moronic architects, or engineers, or whatever the hell they're called who made the metro such an impenetrable labyrinth that even the smartest person can get lost. He hurls himself down the corridor where the young man is still playing (he hardly notices that the Gypsy has gone), turns a couple of corners, bumping into everyone coming in the opposite direction, goes down some stairs, up some other stairs, and again, again, again...

Suddenly everything seems very silent. Even the train that emerges with a whistle from the black cavern on his right seems to arrive in slow motion; it opens its doors very slowly and the passengers seem to float off or on. The Gypsy woman who was begging in the corridor is here now, at the end of the platform, retrieving the packet of handkerchiefs he threw in the litter bin; she smiles and then disappears. The train whistles, closes its doors, and off it goes; as it ponderously gathers speed, he looks again at the message repeated above all the passing doors; he sits there like a doll, watching a sort of endless ribbon: OUTLET THEPASSENGERSOUTLETTHEPASSENGERSOUTLETTHEPASSENGERSOUT. A growing anxiety is taking hold of him; he feels oppressed by the walls, the floor, the curved roof from which the cables are hung, the rails below, shiny against the oil-stained concrete and the sleepers. He looks at everyone else with the envy of the condemned man seeing others as privileged beings able to enjoy something he is about to lose; everyone is going somewhere, they all arrive and they all leave, but he's still there, in the same place he reached a few minutes earlier and where he first saw the advertisements, the benches, the vending machines, the attendant who, with no change of posture (that seems incredible!), is still reading his newspaper. A lump forms in his throat and he begins to cry, wishing now that he had held on to at least one of those handkerchiefs he bought; but they were all taken away by the Gypsy with the strange smile and the sleeping baby wrapped in a brightly coloured shawl.

Mechanically, like a toy horse on a merry-go-round, he sets off again along his route, down the corridor that leads to the Calle Mayor exit. The guitarist is there, faithful to his niche in the cosmos; strangely, he doesn't look like a rebel without a cause, or a vagabond in search of adventure: he's a young man, he doesn't have particularly long hair, his shoes are clean, and he's wearing Terylene trousers; he plays the guitar very well, performing with great concentration and without taking his eyes off the frets, a tune reminiscent of fairground carousels, which helps the passenger walk around a couple of corners, in time to the music, paying no attention to anything else, just going down one set of stairs and up another, and to reappear like a lifeless doll on that same eternal platform: advertisements for an airline, shoes, and a soft drink; benches, litter-bins, and chewing-gum machines; the attendant reading his newspaper; people. A melody sounds in the passageway behind him, and in the distance, to his right, roaring out of the tunnel like a dragon, the two front lights of the train exercise a strange attraction on him, like a mysterious magnet hypnotizing him and making him take a few steps towards the edge of the platform, as though he were dancing.

Translated by Annella McDermott

Fallen from Fortune

Javier Marías

They had told me so that I would be forewarned:

'The Lambeas have fallen from fortune.'

This could mean various things, or so I chose to think after hearing that one phrase over the phone, just that and nothing more, and I was conscious that I should not ask too many questions. Not that I would have been allowed to, even if the person speaking had been there with me, face to face. They tended to be ambiguous in the first instance, and in the last, as if they were merely playing at being criminals, except that sometimes the game grew serious and they turned out to be criminals after all. This happened only on very few occasions, it's true, and on those occasions it was never very clear precisely what had happened, for their preferred scenario was an accident, a suicide, an improvised brawl, or an unfortunate encounter in the street, rather than a murder that could only possibly be a murder and admitted of no other explanation—*what bad luck*—they might say, or, glibly—*well, that's life*—or regretfully—*how awful, how very unfortunate.* Fortune was the word that preceded all others, for you had to fall from fortune in order to be judged unfortunate, and we fall from fortune as if into something that wraps about us, an open hand that tells us of our fate and then closes round us or swallows us up and possibly tightens its grip. But I, not the interested parties or quarry, was the person to whom this announcement had been made, and I was not supposed to pass it on.

I ventured just one question, couched in the most general terms possible, because I was sure that any second question would receive no answer, or at most, a snort of impatience, an unspoken reprimand, a rap across the knuckles for being slow or impertinent.

'And what does that mean exactly?'

'It means that if anything should happen to them during the next day or so, you're not to go out of your way to help them.'

Then the person hung up without saying goodbye, without giving me the chance to find out what I most feared at that moment, to find out if, by some misfortune, *I* was what might happen to them, if *I* was to be that gripping hand. I assumed not, since they would surely have said so more explicitly. I felt slightly relieved, insofar as this was possible, given the ominous nature of the news. When they made this announcement, the first day of that 'day or so' was almost over, for I was to spend only two days accompanying the Lambeas, at their disposal as local contact, interpreter, entertainer, and guide. I was not to leave them alone unless they requested it and was always to remain on hand to resolve any difficulty or problem they might have and to anticipate any possible glitches, making sure, for example, that they didn't arrive at the Prado just as it was closing, that they went to good restaurants, to the shops or to a show, that they were not ripped off or, of course, mugged in the more touristy Habsburg parts of Madrid. Plus, of course, I was to protect them with my presence. Now I was being told to neglect that task, the task of protecting them that is; I was not, however, being ordered to withdraw my presence. Everything, therefore, should continue with apparent normality, and I simply had to wait, to wait until something happened, probably while they were under my guardianship or in my safe keeping. I would have to be a witness, I would be obliged to be there and not to intervene or lend them a hand.

I did not like this warning at all, and not just because of what it meant. Some misfortune would perhaps—for it was not yet certain—befall the Lambeas. But only I knew this, and it fell to me, therefore, to experience the corresponding fear, the state of involuntary, continuous alert. For a second, I wished that the catastrophe would take concrete shape at once, that it would happen now, and thus put an end as quickly as possible to the waiting and to that sense of dread. This desire, however, was immediately succeeded by a hope, that the hours would slip by swiftly and that the moment would come to take them to the airport, to say goodbye, without anything having happened, nothing bad I mean. I did not delude myself though, I had immediately to discount part of that hope: after the phone call, time would pass very slowly indeed.

Giovanni and Sara, that was what the Lambeas were called. Early on, they had invited me to call them by those names and asked if they could do likewise and address me, too, by my first name. I said that they could and, in turn, did as they requested, although I continued to use the formal mode of address; I would have found it very hard not to, even though they were more or less the same age as me—he was perhaps two years older and she two years younger, but after about the age of thirty-five, such differences barely count. He had very pale, watery eyes, as if tears were constantly welling up in them around the edges, and he wore a neatly trimmed, fair beard and was always trying to demonstrate how witty and original he was; personally, I didn't find him funny at all. She was an elegant, serenely attractive woman, with green eyes softened by long, doll-like eyelashes and with a ready, if shy smile, or perhaps she herself reined that smile in; and she treated him with a mixture of devotion and exasperation. It was as if she were profoundly irritated by the foolish things he said, but was, at the same time, devoted to him, to his health and to his humour, as if, on some now distant day perhaps, she had made a huge biographical and emotional investment in Giovanni and had forbidden herself, under any circumstances, to lose him, be it through neglect, insult, illness or accident, let alone death. All her fervour, however, seemed to have less to do with her present-day love for him and more with the momentous decision taken in that remote past. In a sense, Sara reminded me of one of those mothers who do not really like their children, whether young or grown-up, who seem to them to be complete and utter idiots, but from whom they would be incapable of withdrawing their affection or concern; indeed, their heart turns over whenever they see them threatened by some predicament or danger, a mutinous, resentful, even infuriated leap of the heart when it is the umpteenth danger or predicament those children have brought upon themselves or got themselves into, usually some entirely unnecessary and easily avoidable act of folly. And Giovanni, in turn, reminded me of one of those cute kids who always requires the presence of an alarmed spectator, someone to be embarrassed or startled by his crazy ideas and his frank or rude or impertinent remarks, someone who will reproach and reprove him, even if only with a weary, green-eyed glance, which is all he needs in order to know that he has been noticed and has caused pain and created some upset or sorrow. Giovanni was a past master at evincing various tut-tuttings and deep sighs from Sara and at making her too easily frightened pulse quicken.

We were having supper when I got the call on my mobile phone, in the garden of the Iroco restaurant, appallingly badly lit, you can't see a thing, but that was where they had wanted to go or, rather, Giovanni had, since he felt not the slightest curiosity about Spanish food, preferring to dine in a familiar Italian restaurant, whose leafy terrace some acquaintance or some advertising flier had recommended for a late spring or summer evening, though the night had turned chilly and it would have been more sensible to eat indoors, but, in minor matters, Giovanni never missed an opportunity to take the contrary view or to invent whatever new whims circumstances offered him, or to have Sara catch cold and, above all, to worry about him catching cold. Most of the early diners had abandoned their tables and gone inside as soon as the breeze got up, but we had remained almost alone in the gloom, for the light of that late evening or laggardly night was as yet brighter than that provided by the electric lamps. He thought it madness to dine at ten, indeed, he thought the whole Spanish timetable mad, and couldn't understand why we ate so late and why we made everything last such a long time.

From that moment on, as soon as I hung up, everything began to seem dangerous to me, the present, the future, and even, retrospectively, the past. Suddenly, I sensed menace in the slow, hovering darkness, as well as in our momentary solitude in the open air, with occasional gusts of wind that obliged us every so often to hold down the tablecloth and the napkins; and even the waiter who came over from time to time struck me as slightly sinister. I thought, at once, that, instead of walking back to the Hotel Palace where they were staying (it was a pleasant night for walking, but not for sitting outside; the Lambeas had been given a suite, which meant that, before this sudden fall from fortune, they had enjoyed the status of privileged guests; I couldn't imagine what it was that had been unearthed about them), it would be best to take a taxi, although an accident in a car always tends to be more serious than any accident on foot, unless, of course, a pedestrian is knocked down by a car. And a bus or a truck could easily run them over, but leave me unharmed, whereas a collision when all three of us were on board might well carry me off too, and they wouldn't risk that, I didn't think; I'm too useful to them. Then I wondered if I really was that useful and decided that no one ever is.

There was, I told myself, no reason to change the programme for the following morning: while Lambea went about his business and attended various political meetings, which was the reason for his visit, fitting in a bit of lightning tourism along the way, I would take Sara to the Prado, and to the Museo Thyssen-Bornemisza as well if Giovanni took longer than expected and if she felt like it—it's hard to imagine dangers when one is surrounded by pictures and other people. Afterwards, the three of us would have an early lunch at the hotel or in a nearby brasserie. We wouldn't stray very far from that area, which was well guarded because of the adjacent Parliament buildings, and so it was unlikely that anything would happen there, although I had a sudden recollection that, two or three years ago, in summer, in a narrow street immediately behind the Congress building, a Greek tourist, a woman, had grappled with some very young muggers who were trying to steal her handbag, and her assailants had stabbed her, and she had returned to her country with change purse and lipstick intact, but without

her life, all because she had refused to let go of her purse, a
tragic case. Anything could happen anywhere. Perhaps
I should, though, change our plans for the afternoon
and not take them to the Escorial—an hour's drive there
and another hour back, and all for a massive pile of
stones—nor for a stroll through old Madrid, they
wouldn't see the Palacio Real, the ghastly Almudena—
the hideous modern cathedral, best missed anyway—and
the Plaza Mayor, again no great loss nowadays, ever more
degraded, a modern-day Court of Miracles, full of beggars
covered in pustules or bereft of arms, cynical pedlars
manning municipal stalls, lethargic African vagabonds,
or even battle-hardened Slavs, the latter all too often
with bottle in hand; our various mayors have turned the
square into a perpetual circus. If I restricted the Lambeas'
movements as much as possible perhaps nothing would
happen to them during their stay, or what remained of it.
Perhaps I would be able to escort them safe and sound to
their evening flight, and then others in their own country
would be the ones to cause or bring about their misfortune; there would still be plenty of time, and I would not
have to see it, nor feel myself half, or more than that,
three-quarters responsible.

I had grown used to the initial idea that I should
protect them. Not from anything in particular at first,
from the minor incidents that await any foreigner who

does not know the lie of the land—very few are as unlucky as that possessive Greek woman. Also I found it hard to change my attitude and to wilfully neglect them, for the warning had arrived when I had already spent many hours in their company, and you get fond of almost anyone when you know that their presence, your contact with them, will soon end, and that you will never see them again, as if, after that brief encounter, you had, as far as each of you was concerned, died. Sometimes, those encounters become artificially quite intense or intimate, the way unexpected conversations on trains used to in the old days or in the even older days of passenger boats; if you know that someone is about to disappear at any second, nothing seems of great consequence.

My greatest moment of intimacy was with the woman, with Sara, the following morning, while Lambea was busy with his own affairs, and I wondered if, when he returned, he would have some inkling or suspicion that he had fallen from fortune. She and I were in the Prado, and since it is one of those museums where they gratuitously change everything around every few months and where it is impossible to head straight for one particular object without first making enquiries as to its whereabouts, we were wandering aimlessly, stopping in front of any paintings that attracted her attention. She had paused before a full-length portrait of some ghastly little prince; I went over to read the label,

Carlos II, by Juan Carreño de Miranda, it said, the prince who was known as 'el Hechizado'—'the Bewitched or Accursed'. I seemed to recall having seen another even more macabre portrait of him, just head and shoulders, painted when he, the king or prince, was older, an adult, looking even sicklier and, indeed, accursed. In the painting before us we could—alas for him—see his skinny legs, which were not on view in the other painting which I thought I remembered. The long, lank, fair hair falling onto his black-clad shoulders; the face drained of all colour apart from the pale red of his ugly, protuberant lips above that prognathous, almost curved jaw; the huge, dark rings under his eyes—and he was still only an adolescent—eyes that were dull, watery, and slightly bulging; the eyebrows so fine as to be non-existent. He, I thought, had been born into misfortune.

'Why ever did they paint him,' said Signora Lambea, 'given the way he looked?' She too had come over to find out from the label who he was. It said *Carlos II*, therefore he must already have been king by then. 'It seems pointless having a portrait painted of someone so odd and ugly. Even if he was the king.' She was staring at him more with astonishment than repugnance or pity. 'Besides, since he was king, no one could have forced him to exhibit himself like that. They might at least have waited until he looked a bit healthier.'

'I don't know,' I said, just to say something. 'I've seen another portrait of him, in reproduction, painted when he was older, and he looks the same or even worse, he probably never looked healthy. Perhaps *not* painting him would have been tantamount to admitting that the king was hideously ugly. Perhaps, as long as no one actually said as much, he could enjoy the illusion that he wasn't. Sometimes, behaving as if things aren't the way they are makes them less so. At least for a time, at least while those things or people exist, during their present existence. When they cease to be and a few months have passed, everyone tells the truth, but not before, and the fictions continue for as long as is deemed appropriate. You just have to look at your own country. The current pope, for example, has the face of a very nasty man, something on which almost everyone agrees and comments on in private. But no journalist or TV presenter or Vatican pundit will say as much, because it's assumed that every pope is kind-hearted, and they can't allow one pope, even if he isn't kind-hearted, to appear in any other light in the common eye, the eye of the people. So if no one gives explicit expression to that view, however generally held it might be, the same people who see apparent evil in him can pretend that they see only kindness, which is as it should be, and they might even end up believing it and decide that they were wrong from the start. Do you see what I mean?' I added doubtfully. 'I tend to get in a tangle with words, I'm not very good at talking.'

But Sara was clearly hardly listening to me at all, being absorbed in her own thoughts and studying the painting with some distaste.

'It's as if they had painted a portrait of Giovanni when I first met him.' I thought that perhaps the watery eyes and the fair hair had made her associate the two men, except that Lambea was attractive, at least he would be to some women; I thought he was an imbecile. 'He was very ill, you see. You could say that I saved his life. At the time, he looked almost as grim as this young man, whose portrait is fixed here for all eternity. That's how he's been seen and will continue to be seen for centuries. He looks really healthy now, my husband, that is. Really fit. He could have his portrait painted now, but not then. It would have been cruel.'

'In what sense did you save his life? You're not a doctor, are you?'

It seemed to me that Sara blushed very slightly, perhaps regretting having expressed herself so openly, so frankly. But that meant this was the idea she had internalized and believed, although she probably rarely put it into words. She hastily explained:

'No, of course I didn't literally save his life. The doctors did that. But I was the one who persuaded him to go to them, to various doctors overseas—we travelled to three different countries, you know, until we could find a doctor who would give us some hope. I was the one who gave him the necessary tenacity, the one who was with him every step of the way, when he had the transplant and afterwards too, during the long spells in hospitals, during tests and more tests, check-ups and more check-ups; I was the one who gave him hope and strength and encouraged him to go on living. And I'm the one now who tries to make sure he doesn't overdo things and looks after himself as he should. He doesn't take much notice of me, he thinks there's no need, he often puts himself at unnecessary risk. But if I wasn't here, he would probably be dead.'

So that was the biographical rather than emotional investment that Sara Lambea had made. Enough, I thought, for her to remain with her husband and treat him as if he were made of porcelain. It's enough to believe that someone else's life depends on your presence for you not to deny it to them, for you not to feel free simply to leave at any moment, however sick you are of his or her company and of your day-to-day life. It was that mixture of devotion and exasperation that I had noticed in her from the start. The devotion belonged to the past and had spread or continued beyond its birth, growth, explosion, duration, and entire lifespan. Indeed, it must have died a long time ago and given way to the exasperation which belonged to the present and, very likely, to the future. And yet there she remained, chained like a ghost, her extinct devotion surviving after death, like those ancient portraits of patriarchs who preside indefinitely over the rooms of houses, sometimes for generations, watching their descendants, the near and the remote, with a grave or disapproving or harsh expression on their face. Or like the portrait of a king that no one removes. Inside the jokey, capricious, irritating, present-day Giovanni, the helpless, docile Giovanni lived on, the one who had been ill, even terminally ill, the one who would have asked for compassion and help and would have persuaded Sara that she was vital to him, that she was his salvation, and always would be. Maybe she was or maybe she wasn't at all, but some persuasions take such deep root that, afterwards, not even the persuader can root them out.

'When was that?' I asked. 'When did you meet and when was the transplant? What sort of transplant was it?'

'It's getting on for twelve years ago now.' That was all she said.

More than enough time for the mission, begun then, to have expired, but more than enough time, too, for Sara to have become incapable of renouncing it. The only person who could perhaps do that was Giovanni. He doubtless felt well, cured, he would have deliberately forgotten about that pilgrimage of hope and those far-off days of fear, and all that remained, perhaps, was the habit of worrying Sara, of frightening her and keeping her in a state of perpetual alarm. The habit of feeling very loved by her, of having someone concerned about every step he took and his every refusal to obey. And the habit, too, of not cancelling her investment.

When he returned from his meetings and joined us at our table in the brasserie, I noticed that he was somewhat bad-tempered and irritable, less idiotically cheerful than he usually was. But he did not seem depressed or anxious or fearful. Things had clearly not gone as he had wanted, but that would not have led him to infer that he had fallen from fortune or that anything bad was going to happen to him, because they would have put on a front while he was there. When I thought this in the singular, referring only to him, I recalled that the warning had been unequivocally plural: 'The Lambeas', the voice had said. 'The Lambeas have fallen from fortune.' I wondered why her as well, when she hardly seemed to play any role at all in her husband's business affairs, although she was not perhaps entirely ignorant of them, since taking care of them would surely, given the circumstances, have been part of her duties from the beginning. 'Perhaps it's just to make sure there's no one left to make a fuss afterwards or to investigate too closely,' I thought, 'no one to ask questions or to bother themselves about it.' They obviously didn't have children, otherwise Sara would not have been able to behave in that impatient, maternal, nurse-like way towards Giovanni. 'Or perhaps they don't want to leave her alone in the world with no mission to fulfil, in a world grown suddenly empty.' But I did not think my bosses would be quite that considerate.

The morning had passed without problems or upsets; in fact, a day and a half had passed since they had landed in Madrid and some fifteen hours since the ominous warning, and as there were only another eight hours until their departure, I would have to use extreme caution in filling those hours and getting through them. The few steps that Sara and I had taken through the streets—across the Paseo del Prado as far as the museum and back, little more than that—had been a brief torment. I saw an assailant in every person we came across, in every car a potential missile or collision, in every roadworks (of which there are always thousands in Madrid) an accident, a trap, in the museum guards, tourists, and waiters, potential and diverse hired assassins. 'I can't intervene,' I thought before each imaginary danger, 'or I shouldn't. If they're going to kill them, I won't stop them doing so. If something falls on them from some scaffolding, I must let it fall and hit its target.' I had nursed the vague hope that Giovanni would not return from his appointments, that he would meet with an accident on his own, while I was not there, and that his wife might then escape. I had even considered phoning up in order to intercede discreetly on her behalf, to ask if she could not be spared, were anything in fact to happen to them during their time in my care. I disliked Giovanni, but had grown to quite like Sara, nothing more than that, perhaps because of her prolonged efforts on his behalf, or perhaps because I appreciated her serene, green, easily startled eyes. However, I knew that such an initiative would be both unpleasant to undertake and unwelcome. I realized suddenly that my position during the hours to come was not dissimilar to Sara's as regards her husband: if I withdrew my presence, they would be at greater risk, I would leave them more exposed. If I was, according to the order given or the expression used, 'not to go out of my way to help them', it would be best if I did not even attempt to do so, that I simply wasn't there when it happened. But it is enough to believe that someone's life depends on your presence for you not to deny it to them and not to feel free simply to leave, or not entirely. If I did not stand aside, perhaps everything would be more difficult, and they would at least survive until they returned to Rome.

That was when the phone rang, it had been strangely silent for fifteen hours, it was only used by one line, I used my own for other calls. It was an order for me to stand aside.

'When the time comes, don't go with them to the airport,' the familiar voice said. 'Put them in a taxi and invent an excuse, but save yourself the trip. And tell the driver not to go too fast, tell him the lady and gentleman get car-sick.'

I hung up or they did—they were always very succinct—and I imagined what would happen; they would call in the Peruvians or the Colombians. Gangs of men from Peru and Colombia, and from other countries too, sometimes use their car or cars to block the path of another car travelling to or from the airport, or else they insistently honk their horn until the other driver stops; they like new arrivals best and those about to leave, because they have nice, full suitcases. They resort to some subterfuge or to a false alarm to force them to stop and turn off the road, then they escort or guide them to some piece of waste ground and relieve them of their bags. They don't usually kill them, and because they don't leave their cars until they've covered their faces, there is rarely any proof brought against anyone. But then one never knows quite how such things will end, these partial or brief kidnappings. Giovanni, being rash by nature, would be capable of confronting them or pretending to do so, and that would give them the excuse, if they needed one, to kill him; and the taxi driver's version—because they would leave him alive to tell the tale—would be of a robbery that had turned nasty.

And so for a while I stopped worrying—in a manner of speaking—and felt quite happy to take the Lambeas for a stroll around the centre, to see the Palacio Real and the Jardines de Sabatini and the Campo de Moro and the ghastly cathedral, the ruined Plaza Mayor, and the streets in which Calderón de la Barca, the Princess of Éboli, Lope de Vega, and Cervantes had lived and where Escobedo had been murdered. Sara said she found it interesting, but Giovanni didn't care either way, he was still in a bad mood and kept complaining, so much so that when, on this second late evening or laggardly night, I helped them take their somewhat empty bags down to the taxi rank at the Hotel Palace, or, rather, told the bellboy to do so, I felt glad for a moment that I was never going to see them again. It was only a moment because I still wasn't entirely sure that I would not go with them, I mean that I would not, in the end, decide to get in the taxi as well, despite the instructions given by that familiar telephone voice. I had already made my excuses, I had warned them that I couldn't possibly go with them, that an unexpected and very pressing matter had come up, and that, besides, they would have no problems at the airport, there would be people there who could advise them if necessary, the taxi driver would help them with their few bits of luggage, I would take care of that and pay for the trip beforehand and note down the driver's licence plate and number; they were not to worry. (And I would have to note those numbers down anyway in order to pass them on; although someone would already have done so, there was sure to be someone watching.) Sara understood at once ('That's fine, you've done far too much for us already,' she said), but Giovanni seemed put out, he was used to being made to feel important from the moment he got up until the moment he went to bed, especially if he was a guest on a trip abroad. Or perhaps it seemed only logical to him, a consequence of not having reached an agreement or of not having his expectations or desires met. He certainly did not believe that he had fallen from fortune, only perhaps that he had given ground, lost influence. He must think both were still recoverable, any day now: being vain, he was also an optimist.

The luggage had been loaded into the taxi, and I was still unsure what to do. They said goodbye, they thanked me for everything, Giovanni mechanically, Sara with the easy warmth with which one says goodbye to certain essential strangers, to those, that is, who were strangers one or two days before and who are about to become strangers again, as if they had never existed. If we were to meet in six months' time in another context, at an airport, for example, she would not even recognize me; that is how things are. But at that moment, she was almost effusive, she kissed me on the cheek, with a warmth that was neither compromising nor significant. I regretted being always that, an essential stranger, although her 'always' would doubtless prove very brief.

He got into the taxi before her, perhaps out of consideration for her tight skirt or out of irritation or haste. There was still time for me to get in beside the driver and exclaim: 'What the hell, I'll come with you; it won't delay me that much.' But I said nothing, and a tiny hope crossed my mind: 'It's unlikely anything will happen to them, highly improbable really,' I said to myself. 'There's always so much traffic on the way out to Barajas that it would be difficult for someone to intercept them, it would cause an instant traffic jam or an accident and the whole operation would fail, they probably only do that kind of thing on minor roads.' But I also thought that if it wasn't the Peruvians or the Colombians, they would invent something else. At the very last moment, I was just about to open the car door, so as not to deny them my presence or not to be entirely a stranger. My hand was even reaching for the handle, hesitantly and without actually reaching it, when I saw the taxi start up and begin to move off, with the former patient and his eternal nurse on board. The backs of their heads grew smaller as the taxi drove away and I thought: 'Please don't let her turn round to wave goodbye.' When they were still only a short distance away, they had to stop at the lights. And then, with a feeling of dread, I saw her turn her head for an instant and, for the penultimate time, saw those bright, devoted eyes.

There was no way that I could stay then. I raised one arm, I called out, walked swiftly towards the taxi, almost ran, trusting that the lights would not change until I had reached them, although they were sure to wait for me anyway, for she had seen me make that gesture. Then I did open the front passenger door and take my seat beside the driver, and I said to the Lambeas:

'What the hell, I'll come with you; it won't delay me that much.'

The car started off again as soon as I had closed the door. I stared ahead. Whatever would happen would happen, probably even with me there in the taxi. What was new and almost certain is that I, too, had now fallen from fortune.

Personality Disorders

Juan José Millás

The next few days will see the first anniversary of the strange disappearance of my friend Vicente Holgado. Autumn had arrived shortly before in the form of a little warm rain, which had left in the parks and in people's hearts a somewhat rhetorical dampness, equally favourable to sadness and euphoria. My friend's state of mind oscillated between those two extremes, but I attributed this emotional instability to the fact that he had just stopped smoking.

Vicente Holgado and I lived next door to each other in an apartment block in Calle de Canillas, in the Prosperidad district of Madrid. We met one day in rather unusual circumstances, when, overcoming my natural shyness, I knocked on his door to protest not so much about him having his record player on at full volume, but about the fact that he only ever played Simon and Garfunkel, a duo I had adored until Vicente Holgado moved into the neighbouring apartment, which had, until then, been inhabited on and off by a soldier, who had died unexpectedly one weekend, while visiting his home village, of an overdose of bean stew. Vicente invited me in and listened with a certain ironic calm to my complaints, as he poured us each a whisky and put on a video of Simon and Garfunkel's concert in Central Park, New York. I stayed to watch and we became friends.

It would be difficult to sum up his eccentric personality in a few lines, but I will try, even if only to give him a context, to provide the background against which his inexplicable disappearance (well, inexplicable for some) took place. He was the same age as me, thirty-nine, and the only son of a family whose genealogical tree had been so cruelly pruned either by fate's shears or by impotence that it now had no lateral branches. Shortly before moving to Calle de Canillas, he had lost his father—who had been a widower for several years—and was thus suddenly left with no family at all. However, despite this, he still did not seem to be a happy man. Nor could I state categorically that he was manifestly miserable, but his nostalgic voice, his generally sorrowful air, and his sad eyes all suggested a somewhat low-energy character which I, nevertheless, found most attractive. I soon came to realize that he had no friends and no need to work, because he lived off the rents from the three or four large apartments inherited from his father. There were no books in his apartment, only vast quantities of records and video tapes arranged in orderly ranks on purpose-built shelves. The television, therefore, occupied pride of place in that narrow, impersonally furnished living room, at one end of which was a hole that we referred to as the kitchen. His apartment was an exact replica of mine, and given that one was the prolongation of the other, they maintained a troubling mirror-image relationship.

I should also mention that Vicente Holgado only ate sausages, low-fat yoghurts, and sliced bread, and that he went shopping a couple of a times a week attired in the plaid slippers he wore at home and a pair of plain pyjamas, over which he wore a raincoat that reminded me of those worn by flashers in cartoons.

One day, when I returned from work, I couldn't hear Vicente's record player or his television or any of the other noises produced by him moving about the small apartment. The silence lasted for the rest of the day, and so by the time I went to bed, I was starting to get worried and couldn't sleep. The fact is I missed him. The mirror-like relationship between his apartment and mine had recently broadened out to include us.

So at night, when I was cleaning my teeth in my bathroom, separated from his by a thin partition wall, I would imagine Holgado on the other side of my mirror also brushing his teeth. And when I drew back the sheets in order to go to sleep, I visualized my friend performing exactly the same movements and at the same time. If I got up to go to the fridge to get a glass of cold water, I imagined Vicente opening the door of his fridge just as I was opening mine. I even came to think that my dreams were a reflection of his; this was, I believe, simply a way of relieving the loneliness that such apartments inflict on those who live in them for longer than a year. I have yet to meet an inhabitant of a narrow, carpeted apartment who has not developed some serious personality disorder between the first and second year of entering the kind of attenuated death that comes from living in a box.

Anyway, I got up in the night and knocked on his door. No answer. The following day, I did the same, with identical results. I tried to explain his absence to myself by arguing that perhaps he'd had to leave Madrid urgently, but this excuse was simply not credible, given that Vicente Holgado loathed travelling, and that his wardrobe consisted of seven or eight pairs of pyjamas, three pairs of slippers, two dressing gowns, and the aforementioned flasher's raincoat, in which he would go down to the shop or to the bank to withdraw the little money on which he appeared to subsist, but in which he could not have gone much further without attracting unwanted attention. It's true that he did once admit to owning a suit, which he would put on whenever he ventured to travel (his word) into other areas of the city in search of videos, but the truth is I never saw him wearing it. Indeed, shortly after we met, he delegated this responsibility to me, because near my office was a video club where I would rent the videos that we watched together in the evenings.

So, the idea of him having gone off on some urgent journey simply didn't wash.

On the fourth day, I went down to see the porter and told him of my concern. He had a duplicate key for every apartment in the block, and since he knew that Vicente Holgado and I were friends, it was fairly easy for me to persuade him to go with me to Vicente's apartment and find out what was going on. Before putting the key in the lock, we rang the bell repeatedly. Then we decided to open the door, and discovered to our surprise that the safety chain was on and that it could, of course, only be attached from inside. Through the narrow opening allowed by the chain, I called Vicente several times, but received no reply. A feeling of unease or a fear difficult to describe began to fill the area of my body that forensic scientists refer to as the intestinal package. The porter reassured me by saying:

'He can't be dead. If he was, we'd be able to smell him.'

Back in my apartment, we called the police station in Calle de Cartagena and explained the situation. Shortly afterwards, three policemen arrived with a search warrant. One fairly gentle push was all it took to make the chain give way, and we rushed into my friend's apartment like people arriving late for a concert. There was no sign of anything untoward in the living room or in the small bedroom. The policemen looked under the bed, inside the built-in wardrobe, in the fridge. Nothing. The most surprising thing, though, was that the apartment's only two windows were also locked from inside. We were confronted by what cognoscenti of the detective novel call the locked room mystery, which consists of placing the victim of a crime in a room in which all means of escape have been locked from within. In our case, there were no victims, but the problem was the same, because we couldn't understand how Vicente Holgado could have left his apartment having first locked all the windows and doors from the inside.

During the days that followed these strange events, the police kept pestering me; they never explained why they were suspicious of me, although I imagine the mere fact of living alone and being friends with a man like Holgado was more than enough to raise all kinds of conjectures in those accustomed to the many daily manifestations of the weird produced by a city like Madrid. A few newspaper reports appeared as well, but most ended with some supposedly droll comment about the personality of the disappeared man. The porter, to whom I thereafter ceased to give his monthly tip, contributed to making the whole affair still more grotesque by offering his views on my friend's character.

After a time, the police forgot about me and, I suppose, about Vicente too. His file is doubtless stored away in some official basement under the ample section headed 'unsolved cases'. I, however, have not grown used to his absence, which I find all the more painful because Vicente's apartment remains in exactly the state in which he left it. The judge in charge of the matter has not yet decided what should be done with his belongings, despite pressure from the owner who, as is only logical, wants to rent it out again as soon as possible. I find myself, then, in the painful position of having to look at myself in a mirror that no longer reflects back my image. My movements, my desires, my dreams no longer have their duplicate on the other side of the wall; and yet the context in which that duplication took place remains intact. The only thing that has disappeared is the image, the figure, and the representation, unless one accepts that I am the representation, the figure, and the image, and that Vicente Holgado was the original object, which makes me a mere shadow without any real existence. Oh dear.

It is perhaps precisely that growing sense of abandonment and isolation that lies behind my decision to make public something that I chose to conceal at the time, in part so as not to further besmirch my friend's memory and, in part, out of fear that my reputation as a normal person—created after many years of effort and concealment—should in some way be impaired.

I am sure this public statement will bring me all kinds of problems socially, at work, and within my family, but I know, too, that friendship has a price and that even if this public declaration serves only as an amusement for those who can see no further than their own nose, it will nonetheless be my way of returning the silent affection bestowed on me by Vicente Holgado.

The fact is that, in the weeks prior to his disappearance, Vicente had started to take an exaggerated interest in the built-in wardrobe in his apartment. We were watching TV one evening and getting quietly sozzled on whisky when he said out of the blue:

'Have you noticed that the best thing about this apartment is the built-in wardrobe?'

'It is nice and big,' I replied.

'More than that, it's comfortable,' he said.

I nodded mechanically and continued watching the film. He got up from the sofa, went over to the wardrobe, opened it, and started moving things around inside. After a while, he turned and said:

'Your built-in wardrobe is separated from mine by the thinnest of partition walls. If we made a small hole in it, we could go from one apartment to the other through the wardrobe.'

'Hm,' I responded, intent on following the exploits of the hero on screen.

However, the idea of creating a secret communicating door between our wardrobes aroused in me a curiosity I was very careful not to admit to.

After this, the days passed one after the other, as they usually do, and nothing worthy of note happened, apart from the small—but seamlessly connected—changes in my friend's personality. His centre of interest—the television—was imperceptibly shifting to the wardrobe. He would work away in it while I watched TV, and sometimes he would climb right inside and close the door with a bolt that he himself had fitted. After a while, he would reappear, not with the look of someone who has spent half an hour in a dark place, but like someone who has just stepped off a train, his mind full of new experiences and in whose eyes one can still see the blurred reflection of cities, villages, and people glimpsed on a long journey.

I watched all this with the same respectful silence and mute acceptance with which I had observed other eccentricities of his. Having lost for ever the few friends I had in my youth and having accepted at last that men are born, grow up, reproduce, and die—with the exception of men like me and Vicente, who had not bothered to reproduce in order to cut short the whole absurd process—it seemed to me that I should nurture this last friendship, even though the affection and emotions proper to a friendship were never at the forefront of our relationship.

One day, he finally got up the courage to speak to me, and I have kept secret what he told me then for the whole of this last year in the hope that I might manage to erase it from my mind. To use his words, he had a long-cherished desire that had evolved into a theory, according to which all the built-in wardrobes in the world were connected. And so if you climbed into your own wardrobe and found the necessary conduit, you could arrive in a matter of seconds in a wardrobe in an apartment in Valladolid, to give but one example.

I eyed the wardrobe warily and asked:

'And have you found that conduit?'

'Yes,' he replied in feverish tones. 'I discovered it on the day I realized that the conduit isn't a place, but a state, like hell. I've spent several days visiting the built-in wardrobes of the neighbouring apartments.'

'Why haven't you gone further afield?' I asked.

'Because I'm not yet familiar enough with the mechanisms for coming back. I had a real fright this morning, because I climbed into my wardrobe and suddenly found myself in another one (rather comfortable as it happens) from which I could hear a conversation in an unfamiliar language. Frightened, I tried to come back at once, but it took me ages. I fell from wardrobe to wardrobe until, at last, although I still don't know how, I found myself back here again. You should see the things people keep in their wardrobes and how they neglect them. You'd be amazed.'

'Hm,' I said, 'well, you'd better stick to the local neighbourhood until you've had more practice.'

'Yes, that's what I thought I'd do.'

The day after this conversation, Vicente Holgado disappeared from my life. I was the only person, at least until today, who knew that he had disappeared into the wardrobe. I would like to make an appeal to all people of goodwill, first, to keep their wardrobes neat and tidy, and second, if they should at any time open their wardrobe and find inside it a man wearing a pair of thin pyjamas and with the sad features described above, that will be my friend Vicente Holgado. Please advise me of his whereabouts as soon as possible.

How can this be happening to me?

Carmen Posadas

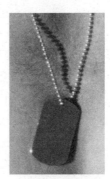

It was a Sunday afternoon, possibly in May, and the city was dozing in the heat of the first really hot sun of the season. Everything appeared to be still, almost deserted, as if the hour and the heat were conducive only to sleep or boredom. Down in the street, a few passers-by were walking briskly along on their way to a cinema or a swimming pool, and up above, on the terrace roofs, all was quiet. *He* occupied one particularly spacious terrace, his naked body reclining on a striped air bed. Abel had one of those powerful bodies with long, shapely limbs, and his head, too perfect even for a Greek statue, crowned a physique that had brought him his fair share of problems.

'Hm, nice,' he would hear women say as he passed or when he was serving coffee at thirty thousand feet or when he put on his flight attendant suit that made him look like a pilot; and he accepted these compliments with the bored air of one who considers himself to be something more than just a well-made body.

Abel's apartment was in one of the districts in the north of the city, where the buildings have grown so tall that the place has started to resemble Manhattan. Well provided with aerials and satellite dishes, his block (sixty luxury apartments with garage, garden, swimming pool, and easy payment terms) competes with its neighbour to be the tallest with the best view of the mountains. And in that rival building, two storeys above him, with the window open to let out the heat, was Lola.

Sunday was Lola's favourite day. Ever since she gave up work, Sundays, for Lola, had positively oozed transgression and made her feel truly blessed, because, for the idle rich like her, the seventh day of the week always has the somnolent slowness of a holiday without the lurking presence of a miserable Monday. It was about three o'clock in the afternoon, and outside, a hot but somewhat hazy sun was shining down, not so feebly as to depress her, but not strongly enough either to make her long to be outside. Lola was looking out of the open window of her brand-new twentieth-floor apartment. Or, rather, she looked out now and then, whenever she glanced up from the manuscript she was checking. A pleasant silence filled every corner; there was no one at home, the telephone was unplugged, and the only sign of life outside was the radio cassette player that the guy on the roof terrace opposite had on at full blast. There they were, alone, the two of them, looking out over an irregular platform of rooftops and deserted roof terraces; her and the naked man toasting himself in the sun to the sound of *Madam Butterfly.*

Very occasionally, a favourable wind would bring other sounds to Lola's ear, like that of a child splashing in some distant swimming pool, and then she would look up and her eyes would invariably drift over to the only animate object in sight, Abel. They had never been formally introduced, but over time and thanks to the indiscretions of porters and cleaning ladies, each had managed to gather quite a lot of unsolicited information about the other. Abel knew, for example, that the blonde woman with whom he sometimes coincided at the traffic lights on the corner was called Lola, that she was thirty-five years old and had just scored a huge literary hit with one of those fat, autobiographical, and incredibly slow novels so adored by certain critics. However, this information only served to confirm that she didn't interest him in the least. 'No spring chicken, a know-all and stuck in her ways. Who's going to want to take a ride on her?'

Lying face down on his air bed, Abel half-closed his eyes and looked up. Something was waving about at one of the high windows of the building opposite, perhaps a curtain, but he didn't see Lola gazing rather dully down on him from above. For she, too, had gleaned some information about Abel and knew that he was one of those shop-window-dummy men, the kind who, whenever a woman looks at him, automatically starts posing and flexing his muscles; he was also (obviously) a *naffus maximus*, the sort who never takes off his Rolex or Cartier watch even when sunbathing naked.

After briefly, and quite disinterestedly, running her eyes over his golden thighs, Lola went back to the manu-script and concentrated on her work. She was checking through what would be her second novel and was using a thick yellow highlighter to mark any mistakes and typos. After almost eighteen months of hard work, this process was pure pleasure, despite the many spelling errors with which the typist had been so kind as to spatter her work.

Suddenly Lola realized that she was feeling very hot. This came upon her suddenly, as it does sometimes, and she fanned herself with some sheets of paper, then opened the window still wider and decided to take off her jeans so that the sun could gently caress her knees. She removed them carefully, slipping them down over her legs with a satisfied smile on her face as she read a particularly well-turned sentence. The rough cloth brushed first her knees, then her ankles, until, finally, she kicked them off. They landed behind a sofa. Then, with a little forward shuffle, she adjusted the polka-dot panties she was wearing under her jeans. Yes, she felt much better like that.

Abel sat up very slowly. He always tried to make his every movement slightly feline, but today, because he was naked, he emphasized this tendency still more. Like many people, he never felt entirely comfortable without clothes, especially when he was on his own; somehow one feels more naked alone than in company. Then, as he struggled against his body's stubborn desire to curl up in a ball, he wondered if such modesty was something relatively new in him, the result of an embarrassing episode that still floated in his memory like a smelly fart. It had happened in Formentera, less than two months ago: he was sunbathing on the beach, when three women came up and started teasing him as if he was, well, a sex object or something. He had tried to laugh it off and pretend that he was in control of the situation, but then the fattest of the three women simply flung herself on top of him, and her intentions were clearly far from honourable. It was a horrible experience, enough to render one impotent for life.

'These liberated women are a real pest,' Abel thought as he let himself be lulled by the music of *Madam Butterfly*. 'They're always trying to draw attention to themselves.'

Lying face down again, he reached out one hand for the sun oil, Tropical Orgy, and then abruptly turned over and adopted a yoga position halfway between sitting and kneeling. The sun glinted on his amber skin while a passing breeze carried the strains of *Madam Butterfly* to Lola so clearly that she looked up. It was hot, very hot, and Lola was playing distractedly with her yellow highlighter. She kept pushing it in and out of her mouth and curling her tongue around the cap. It was a thick highlighter, made in Germany in the form of a prism, and it kept clicking against her teeth. Then she stopped, aware that she was feeling vaguely aroused by the sight of Abel down below on the distant island of his roof terrace, and she concentrated on observing how the sun seemed to penetrate his thighs and draw golden glimmers from them. It only lasted a moment, then the feeling vanished, driven away by one of those pedestrian thoughts that tend to slip into one's mind at the most inopportune moments, like having forgotten to buy the bread or some such thing.

'Oh really...' she said to herself and tried to revive that hint of excitement. She again ran her tongue over the rough surface of the highlighter while she gazed at Abel, who occasionally stretched languidly, and who now seemed to have adopted a new posture, lying on one side, like a magnificent Rokeby Venus, revealing every perfect, lustrous muscle.

'Take a good look, Lola, keep looking.'

But she felt nothing now, the excitement had gone, and, feeling somewhat annoyed, she withdrew a little from the window. Since becoming a famous writer, she had begun to suspect that she was developing the odious habits of a collector of experiences, as if she were no longer capable of feeling, as if by transforming herself into a dispassionate observer of her own and other people's passions, she had lost the ability to be moved. She called it her 'entomological vein'.

'What do you expect?' said a novelist friend, with whom she sometimes went partying and who also figured on the best-seller lists. 'That's what happens to those of us crazy enough to devote ourselves entirely to literature wihout watering it down with a little journalism and other such solvents: we *feel* in order to write. You'll see, it won't just be your libido rusting up, you'll find yourself making mental notes about your every emotion, as if you were a bloody accountant. Love, hate, not to mention orgasms and even terror, you'll have them all neatly labelled so that you can use them later on in a story, in the form of adverbs and adjectives. It's every writer's curse.'

Lola shook her head to rid herself of this idea, and her tongue, as if also wanting to deny such a possibility, again curled itself about the black top of the highlighter. Lola was concentrating now on the movements of Abel's strong hands as he rubbed oil onto his chest. His firm, gleaming body glittered with a thousand golden points, the light catching his thick, fair chest hair. She opened her mouth to take in more air, her lips parted, and the top of the highlighter slipped cleanly past the barrier of her teeth and deep into her mouth, very deep.

There was a hoarse sound, and the inverted plastic pyramid lodged itself behind her uvula.

It did not take her long to realize what had happened, confirmed as this was by her stopped breath and the smell of fear, something she had heard about but never quite believed in. Then she saw little stars of alarm and heard the quickening beat of her heart.

'I'm choking,' she thought incredulously, for an absurd calm allowed her to be as conscious of what was going on as if it wasn't happening to her at all; no, something so terribly stupid couldn't possibly be happening to her. She could see her reflection in the glass of the open window; she was standing up, stiff and erect, but somehow absent too, in her polka-dot panties, and she could even see her own deep, black mouth agape and her fixed staring eyes. This lasted an eternity, until a rather more realistic finger attempted to remove the plastic top, but failed; this at least shook her out of her futile catalepsy.

'Good God!'

And she started to think. She looked out of the window, and nothing appeared to have changed. She was dying, and the sun was still in its place. Down below, far away, in the street, she could make out a few children playing ball, entirely unaware that she was dying, and even over there, in the apartments opposite, behind the windows, someone was playing solitaire—jack, queen, king—as if this were not the end of the world. 'So this is what death is like,' she thought. 'Dying is seeing how the world carries on without you ... If I could only do something, perhaps if I breathed very softly, yes, it feels like a little air is entering my lungs. Keep calm, keep calm, and whatever you do, don't panic. I'm not going to die, these stupid, horrible things only happen to other people, you read about it in the newspapers. "Young woman chokes to death on highlighter top." It's so stupid, stupid, stupid ... Breathe slowly, Lola, keep calm. I know some people have survived this kind of thing, I've read that it can take ages for someone to die of asphyxiation ... that's it, breathe. Oh dear God, how I wish now that you did exist, even if only so that I could put the blame on you. How can this be happening to me? I'm going to go over to the window and climb onto the ledge. If I could only shout or cry out. Surely that man down there will see me. What the hell am I doing, I'll kill myself if I'm not careful, I'm twenty floors up, slowly now, I might stumble, I might fall, but what does it matter if I'm dying anyway and that narcissistic fool isn't even looking. Just a minute. I don't need anyone else, what about the Heimlich manoeuvre, that's the answer. I read about it recently, in *Marie Claire* I think, although what does it matter where I read it? It's a way of expelling foreign bodies from the throat, it's just a matter of putting your arms around the chest of the poor wretch who's dying, in this case me, no, this can't be happening to me. Shut up, Lola ... You put your arms around the dying person's chest and place your clasped hands immediately below the ribcage, like that, and then you push up ... Please work, damn it, or I'll die, but wait, the guy down there is looking up at me, he's seen me. Come on, Lola, hang on in there, just a little longer!'

The sun burning his blue eyes does not prevent Abel from seeing what is going on a few yards up above, in the window of the building opposite. From where he is, the details of the scene are nakedly, absurdly obvious, with the added absurdity conferred by silence and distance. There she is. A woman of thirty-five is doing the unspeakable in order to attract his attention. He can't quite hear, but judging from the way in which she keeps opening and closing her mouth, he would say that she was panting.

Abel frowns to see this woman—yes, it's that snooty blonde woman he's seen at the traffic lights—standing at the window exhibiting herself and wearing only a small pair of polka-dot panties. She's getting worked up now, she's groping her own breasts and not very sexily either. The strange figure's movements grow wilder still, and Abel realizes that, much to his regret, it's time to cover up.

'Women,' he mutters, 'they're all the same.'

From a sports bag he takes a pair of pale blue swimming trunks that he bought last week in New York. He puts them on, having carefully smoothed out any wrinkles, all the while trying not to look up at the window. However, his disobedient eyes do eventually glance upwards. There's no one there.

Abel breathes more easily. He's lying down now with his hands behind his head and he displays himself on his air mattress like some indolent clothed *maja*.

'All right, all right, woman. Maybe I'll call you up one of these evenings and ask you out to supper.'

Manolito's Toggle

Elvira Lindo

At the beginning of September, my mother sent my grandpa and me off to buy a toggle to replace the one missing from my duffel coat. 'Big Ears' López bit it off last year when I refused to give him my sandwich. He broke a tooth, and I was left without a toggle. His mother consoled him for his loss, mine gave me one of those delayed-action slaps on the back of the neck that only start to sting about half an hour later. I learned then that if you want to get on the good side of your mother, you'll get a much better response if you break some part of your body than if you tear your clothes. They really don't like that. And yet, the minute your back is turned, they'll be boasting about their child's latest injury:

'My son broke his leg yesterday.'

'Well, mine split his head open.'

Mothers never like other mothers to get one over on them. That's why, come September, my mother said:

'I don't want you starting school and then find that we're in October already and still haven't sewn that toggle back on your duffel coat.'

It's last year's duffel coat, and it'll be this year's too and the next year's and the next and the next, because my mother says that boys grow a lot and so you have to buy duffel coats with an eye to the future. Some boys may grow a lot, but I don't. That's why this is the duffel coat I'll be wearing when I'm old and dead. I hate my duffel coat, and I'll have to spend the rest of my life hating the same duffel coat. How boring!

This summer, my mother made the doctor prescribe me some vitamins. I think she's embarrassed that my duffel coat is always the same number of sizes too big and she's feeding me these vitamins so that the duffel coat and I will, eventually, be the same size. Sometimes I think my mother cares more about my duffel coat than she does about me, and I'm her own flesh and blood. I asked my grandpa about this when we were going off to buy the toggle, and he said that all mothers get fond of duffel coats and overcoats in general, as well as hats and gloves, but despite this, they still love their children, because mothers have very big hearts.

In the area where I live, Carabanchel, there's a bit of everything, a prison, buses, children, prisoners, mothers, drug addicts, and bakers, but there are no toggles for duffel coats; and so my grandpa Nicolás and I took the metro downtown.

We're always lucky on the metro because, even when it's really full, people take pity on us and offer us a seat. They feel sorry for my grandpa because he's old and has prostate problems. You can't see his prostate, but you can see that he's old. They probably feel sorry for me, too, because I wear glasses, but I can't be sure.

When someone gives up their seat, we have to pretend to be poor grateful wretches, because if, for example, they give you their seat and you sit down and immediately burst out laughing, people get very annoyed. So my grandpa and I always get on the metro looking as if we are on our last legs, and it works every time. Try it, but don't go telling everyone, because word might get round and then that will be that.

My mother had sent us to Pontejos, which is a shop in Puerta del Sol, where mothers from all over the world go to buy buttons, zips, and toggles.

We spent an hour standing at the counter because my grandpa kept letting any lady customers go ahead of him. He loves doing that and he'd like it even better if they'd have coffee with him afterwards. So far, none of them ever has, but he lives in hope.

After we'd been there an hour, with my grandpa talking first to this lady and then to that, I tried to lie down on the counter because I was tired of standing up, and that was when the assistant decided to serve us. He didn't want me putting my boots on his counter, and so once we'd bought the toggle, my grandpa said:

'Right, we've done our duty, Manolito, now let's go for a little stroll along the Gran Vía.'

'Cool, dearest Grandpapa.'

Well, I didn't actually say 'dearest Grandpapa'. If I did, he'd think I'd gone mad and pack me off for some electroshock treatment.

We went to the Gran Vía. And what do you think we saw? A demonstration. We have demonstrations sometimes in Carabanchel too, but they're never as nice as the ones on the Gran Vía. My grandpa said:

'Let's join the crowd.'

The people demonstrating must have thought this was fine, because they didn't chase us away. My grandpa asked a gentleman if he could lift me onto his shoulders so that I could see the man giving the speech. When I was up there, I noticed that the guy had dandruff and so I started brushing it off. I asked him why he didn't buy that shampoo they advertise on telly that not only gets rid of your dandruff, it gets you a gorgeous girlfriend too. The guy removed me from his shoulders (I think he was a bit annoyed) and said:

'He doesn't half weigh a lot, your grandson.'

For a moment, that cruel man gave me a complex about my weight. I always have some complex or other. I've had a complex about my height, my weight, my glasses, and about having two left feet. I won't go on because I don't like to put myself down. Last year, though, I had a really bad complex about my weight, but I got over it when I realized that it was daft to have a complex about being fat when I wasn't.

My grandpa didn't even notice what the guy with the dandruff said. By then, he had started protesting about his pension, which is what he always does when he's with a group of more than two people. He also said that society's gone downhill ever since the introduction of pressure cookers.

We were walking along the street, which was empty of cars. The place was heaving with policemen, though, and I was thinking: 'How cool.' After a while, though, the demonstration ended and then my grandpa said:

'I'm going to buy you a hamburger so that your mother can't accuse me when we go home of starving you to death.'

He bought me a burger and ordered three ice creams, two for him—because of his prostate—and only one for me, because I'm on the chubby side. And I thought: 'How cool is this, man, how coo-coo-cool!' I think it was the most important day in my entire life; I started jumping up and down for joy and my grandpa said:

'Don't do that, you're not allowed to jump up and down in the Gran Vía because the metro runs underneath, and the slightest vibration could bring the whole street crashing in on it.'

I felt a bit embarrassed and jumped up and down mentally instead. I'm used to doing that because otherwise our neighbour, Luisa, comes up and asks if we're having a replay of the San Francisco earthquake or something.

Anyway, I swear that we were just about to go home, when we saw a woman who reads the news on telly sitting in a café eating a chicken, mayonnaise, lettuce, and tomato sandwich. I know this because my grandpa and I stood watching her through the window until she'd finished.

The woman didn't know where to look; you could tell she was embarrassed. At one point, she dribbled a bit of mayonnaise down her chin and quickly wiped it away. She called the waiter over and gestured to him to close the curtains, then got shirty because there were no curtains.

I had to stay until she got up because some of the kids at school say that lots of news presenters have no legs, which is why they become news presenters in the first place, because news presenters don't need legs. My friends would never have forgiven me if I'd left without finding out. And to do that, you have to go downtown, where the famous people are, because in Carabanchel, there are no famous people and no toggles. The waiter came out and said to my grandpa:

'Look, Grandpa, if you want to see animals, take the boy to the zoo. This is a café.'

And my grandpa said straight out:

'I'm standing in the street with my grandson and neither you nor the mayor himself can make me move, even if the mayor were to ask me *en personne*.'

My grandpa came out with that *en personne* just like that; he's never been one for putting on airs. But the waiter didn't give up; he was your typical celebrity creep, and he said:

'It's my responsibility to allow the TV presenter to eat her sandwich in peace and not as if she were a monkey in the monkey house.'

'You're the one who used the word "monkey" not me,' said my grandpa, who can speak better than the President himself when he wants to. 'But I don't know why Madame Presenter should be so bothered about being looked at by a poor old man and a child when, every night, she has millions of viewers hanging on her every word.'

'Well, it does bother her,' said the waiter, who was obviously determined to win first prize for bore of the year and prize celebrity creep.

'Well, it bothers me even more,' said my grandpa to the waiter and to the crowd gathering round us in the Gran Vía. 'It bothers me even more', he said again, 'that Madame Presenter keeps fluffing her lines when she reads the news, because her salary comes out of the taxpayer's pocket, out of *my* pocket, because I still have to pay taxes even though my pension doesn't even run to buying myself a truss. Why doesn't she talk about pensions on her programme?'

When my grandpa said this, the people started applauding more loudly than they had for the guy addressing the demonstrators earlier on. My grandpa's chin was trembling as it always does when he gets over-excited.

People told the waiter to bring him a glass of water, and the waiter had to do as he was told and go back into the bar; but he wasn't the one who came out holding the glass of water.

You're not going to believe this, but I swear on my idiot brother's head that the person who brought him the water was the newsreader herself. This was a key moment in our lives.

'Here you are,' she said in her TV voice. 'Are you feeling better?'

My grandpa said that he was and that he had simply wanted to prove to his grandson that TV presenters have legs, and very pretty ones too, he added, and that there wasn't another newsreader like her and the cameras really didn't do her justice, because she was a hundred times prettier in real life, but he really had to be going now, his grandson would be starting back at school the next day and they'd only come downtown to buy a toggle, and goodness, was that the time, his daughter would probably have phoned the police by now. After finishing this second speech, he took another couple of sips of water and we set off. My grandpa hailed a taxi in the Gran Vía, because it was getting really late. The second lot of telly news would have already been and gone. A taxi stopped, and he said to the taxi driver:

'We're going to Carabanchel Alto. Would six hundred pesetas be enough for the fare?'

And the driver said:

'No it bloody wouldn't. Carabanchel's miles away.'

The driver didn't want to take us and didn't want to leave us either. Some people get annoyed because you ask them a simple question, and some people are just plain nasty.

'After that hamburger, we're down to our last six hundred pesetas, Manolito.'

There he was blaming my hamburger, having quite forgotten that *he*'d wolfed down two ice creams. And so we had to go home the way we came, on the metro.

I started feeling really sleepy, thinking about school, the newsreader, the winter, and my duffel coat. And if, as well as doing all that thinking, you're travelling on the metro, your head gets so heavy you reach the point where you can't even think. My grandpa must have been feeling the same, because he said:

'I'm just going to have a little nap, Manolito. Make sure we don't go past our stop.'

But I fell asleep too, deep asleep, very deep asleep.

A guard woke us; we were out somewhere in the back of beyond and with no idea what time it was. There's nothing worse than falling asleep on the metro and waking up in the back of beyond. I started crying before anyone could tell me off. But the guard didn't tell us off; he explained that we were at Casa de Campo and then travelled with us to our station, probably because he could tell my grandpa had problems with his prostate. When we reached home, all the neighbours were at the front door, consoling my mother over our disappearance. Luisa had told her:

'Don't worry, Cata. If they were dead, it would have been on the news.'

Everyone was furious with my grandpa: what was he thinking of, the child had to get up early, and he'd had no supper, and they'd been just about to call out the special police rescue team. My grandpa raced up the stairs (well, 'raced' is perhaps not the word) to escape the multitude.

When we'd been back home an hour or so and my mother had listed everything we had ever done wrong since the day we were born, it suddenly occurred to her to ask:

'And what about the toggle?'

We couldn't find it anywhere; and then she said that, one of these days, we'd be the death of her.

For the first time since the end of the summer, my grandpa left his socks on in bed; I know this because I shared his bed. Because where I live, in Carabanchel, as soon as school starts, so does the cold. This has been shown to be true by scientists worldwide.

Time passed, then some more time and after the third lot of time, I realized that I couldn't sleep. Tomorrow was the first day of school, and everyone would have so many things to talk about that probably no one would be interested in what had happened to me in the Gran Vía. All this was going on inside my head because I thought my grandpa was asleep, but suddenly I heard him say:

'We had a smashing time this afternoon, didn't we, Manolito? When I tell them at the day centre tomorrow that the newsreader from the telly brought me a glass of water, they won't believe me. Just as well you were there as a witness.'

That was all he said, because then he fell asleep and began breathing through his mouth. He does that because he has to take his teeth out to go to sleep. I heard the radio announcer say something about tomorrow being the first day back at school, something I didn't need reminding about, thank you very much.

Mind you, there were some good things about going back to school: I would see Susana again and 'Big Ears', although I'd spent all summer with him—boring!

Now my grandpa was breathing steadily. I realized that he'd got into bed with his cap on. Whenever something really important has happened, he forgets to take off his cap. Well, at least it would keep his head warm. My grandpa may have no hair on his head and no teeth, but as you'll have noticed, he doesn't mince his words.

I think I was just beginning to fall asleep when I realized that I was holding something in my hand. It was the toggle. I hadn't let it out of my grasp for a moment. My mother could sew it on for me in the morning, then she'd be happy.

This had been the most important day in my life, but it didn't matter: no one could save me from school or winter or my duffel coat. Yes, that was the worst thing: no one could save me from my duffel coat.

Sign and Message

José María Merino

Moya came across Souto one morning in early autumn, in the squalid camp set up by some Africans in Plaza de España. He had just been buying a few tins of cat food and was walking across the square to pick up his watch from a jeweller's in the Torre de Madrid, when he noticed a reddish, bearded face among all the chocolate-brown ones.

Souto had long, dishevelled hair and was sitting indolently on some cardboard on the ground, gazing up at the monument to Cervantes. Moya went closer and observed him intently, just to make sure that this really was the old friend, who, after his sudden departure from academia, had become a legendary figure, a vagabond and the protagonist of many outlandish tales. Pleased to find his colleague again, Moya called out to him, albeit with the respectful caution of one who finds himself before a man who has chosen to live far from his former friends:

'Souto! Professor Souto!'

Souto tore his gaze from the monument and looked at Moya hard, without saying a word, giving no sign of recognition.

'Ah, the beneficent Moya,' he said at last, pronouncing the words very slowly. 'My kindly publisher.'

Moya felt ashamed of Souto's dirty, ragged appearance, clear evidence of the once neat and dapper professor's strange metamorphosis into a tramp. He decided to take him away from the square.

'You're coming back home with me to have a bath and put on some clean clothes,' he said.

Souto did not even get to his feet. He scornfully rejected these proposals as vain and foolish.

'You mean you're going to sleep here?' asked Moya, who was finding his former colleague's situation ever more distressing.

'I'm as free as the air,' retorted Souto. 'I slept here last night, but who knows where I'll wake up tomorrow.'

'But what about food? Have you eaten?' asked Moya, feeling genuinely concerned.

'No, I haven't,' said Souto. 'I haven't eaten anything all day.'

They walked over to Flavio's bar, where the owner eyed Souto with distaste. Souto wanted only a glass of milk and an omelette sandwich, but he did at least seem a little less reserved and distant.

'You're probably thinking that I don't look exactly in the pink, but there you'd be wrong,' he said, munching away rather unenthusiastically. 'Inside, I'm very well indeed, better than ever, in fact. I devote myself entirely to research now, without the bother of dealing with schools or university departments.'

He drank his glass of milk down in one and ordered another.

'Research? What research is that?' asked Moya.

In Souto's eyes there appeared a spark that came perhaps from the crackling bonfire of his memories.

'It's a very long story,' he said at last. 'One day, I got tired of making inventories of phonemes and started analysing natural noises instead. I listened to the voices of animals and the sounds made by water. Everything has its own code. I also considered the shapes of rocks, the lines and notches created by erosion. Everything is a sign, a message. The difficult part is trying to discover what they mean. Contemptible modern-day society rejects any messages that are not trying to sell them something and thus they dig their own grave ever deeper. But that doesn't mean the world isn't still full of signs and symbols.'

Moya felt reassured by Souto's growing animation.

'And what about poetry? Have you gone back to writing poems? That collection of yours was really very good. I sold nearly five hundred copies.'

'Poetry!' cried Souto. 'Poetry has become just another way of obscuring rather than illuminating! It sheds no light at all, although the vacuous bigheads who write it may claim otherwise. All the real poets died hundreds of years ago!'

He tapped his fingers on the table, as if counting out the syllables of a sonnet, then added trenchantly:

'What passes for poetry has become a mere sewer for inanities. I'll never go back to it.'

Moya managed to persuade Souto to accompany him to his office. When the tramp-professor entered the basement room, he looked around in surprise.

'You remember this place, do you?' asked Moya.

'Of course,' said Souto. 'This was the home of the New Science. Think of all the anti-Franco meetings we held here, as many as there were executions by the Inquisition, carried out in this very place in other equally unenlightened times.'

Moya's cats had emerged from their hiding places and were rubbing against him, coiling sycophantically about him.

'Whose cats are these?' asked Souto.

Somewhat embarrassed, Moya explained that they were strays.

'Some I took in when they were nothing but skin and bone after some brute had mistreated them. This one had been run over by a motorbike. He was my first rescue cat, and the others I found along the way. After all, they have a right to live too.'

As he opened a few tins of food for them, the cats formed a purring chorus.

'You see?' said Souto, stroking the back of one of them. 'The message is quite clear: I'm hungry, starving, ravenous.'

'And now?' asked Moya. 'What do you do now?'

For a moment, Souto stiffened as he had when they first met, and Moya thought bleakly that the steady recovery of trust between them was over. This, however, wasn't the case. After a silence, Souto rummaged around among his ragged clothes and produced a bundle of papers, which he placed on the table. Some of the papers bore a large number of scribbles in ballpoint pen.

'Do you recognize them?'

Moya looked puzzled.

'They're copies of the graffiti you find on walls, those anonymous signatures you see all over Madrid. I'm making a catalogue of the ones in this area. I track their evolution and note down any new ones. At first, they were just random unintelligible words, look, pier, dock, dart, hotline, teacher, and then certain names began to appear, tronky, juanmanuel, isidro. But at one point—I have a note of the exact date—in the spring of 1990, I noticed some completely illegible scribbles beginning to appear. They followed one of two patterns: rounded and jagged. Within those two types, it was possible to distinguish between those that had some artistic merit, what I would call designs, and the clumsy efforts of someone merely letting off steam, but it would take me too long to explain all this properly. Later on, a different style emerged, which greatly disconcerted me, because it contained strange lines and dots I had never seen before, and the direction of the strokes was odd too. Nevertheless, I can say with some confidence that I have identified the formal origin of what I refer to as atypical graffiti; some are reminiscent of Xibe or the extinct language of Manchu, others resemble Oriya, and some, although not the most common ones, look like Arabic script.'

The vagabond life had clearly not eroded Souto's professorial abilities. The cats, having eaten, returned to their resting places from which they observed him intently, while Moya listened like an earnest student.

'That's what I'm doing now,' concluded Souto. 'I've set this autumn as my deadline for collecting information, before getting down to work and trying to interpret it all.'

'Well, when you've finished, you can count on me to publish the book,' said Moya encouragingly.

'Oh, I have no interest in publishing my findings,' said Souto loftily. 'I'm not even sure I'm going to set my conclusions down in writing. As I told you, I have abandoned the pomp and the backbiting of academe. I am doing this research purely for my own interest and I don't intend revealing the results to anyone.'

The phone rang, and the call lasted some time. Meanwhile, Souto had gone into the other part of the cellar, which served as the stockroom for books. After that first call, Moya had to make various others, and this kept him busy for more than an hour, during which time Souto had still not emerged from the stockroom.

Moya was sorting through invoices, delivery notes, and other documents when Souto appeared at the door.

'I'd forgotten how many books you'd published,' he said.

'Forgotten!' exclaimed Moya cheerfully. 'They represent more than twenty-five years of Leftist culture. Pure archaeology, given the way things are going.'

'Did you follow a particular order when putting them on the shelves?' asked Souto, and Moya looked at him, bewildered.

'What order would I follow? I put them on the shelves in the order they came back from the printer's, and depending on how much space was left.'

'Well, it's full of strange concatenations,' said Souto, 'as if there were a symbolic meaning in the way the books had been placed, a discourse linking different ideas about solitude, along an axis linking childhood with work and death.'

That was when Moya had the idea. He pressed carriage return on his typewriter and stood up.

'Listen, Souto, I'm not going to take "No" for an answer. You're going to sleep here, on this very sofa, and you can cover yourself with that blanket, if you like. There's a toilet at the back of the stockroom. You can study the order of the books and anything else that takes your fancy. You have paper here, as well as pens, pencils, and felt-tips. Why live out on the street?'

'Don't you understand? I don't want to be tied to anything!' exclaimed Souto. 'These are just new temptations to get me to succumb to corruption.'

'What do you mean "temptations"? The sofa has completely had it, I mean, you can see the springs sticking out, and just look at the state of this blanket. The cats have ruined it.'

'What about the bathroom?' asked Souto in an accusing tone of voice.

'What do you mean "bathroom"? There's a toilet and a small sink with one cold water tap. That's hardly going to corrupt you. But at least you would have a desk to put your papers on when you're busy with your research.'

Souto still wore a very stern expression.

'I don't like people doing me favours. As they say in Latin America, even a saint mistrusts an over-generous gift.'

'Favours? I'm hardly doing you a favour. You can give the cats their supper and save me a daily trek from my house; in fact, most of the time, I can't even be bothered.'

'All right, I'll stay here tonight,' Souto said at last, 'but I'm not promising anything.'

That same evening, it began to rain heavily, and Souto slept in the office that night and the next. A week later, he was still there, although Moya scarcely saw him, because Souto got up very early and was gone most of the day, covering his rags with a military-style greatcoat he'd found among the rubble in a skip. One night, Moya awaited his return, so that he could chat to him and find out how things were going.

Souto arrived at eleven, and Moya could see that the cats had established a real rapport with him.

'I never see hide nor hair of you,' said Moya, 'you're out all day and in all weathers too.'

'Fieldwork,' explained Souto, 'but under cover, in the metro.'

'In the metro?'

Then Souto told him that on the morning after the first night he spent at the office, he had found in the cramped entrance of the nearby metro station Noviciado, near the exit for Calle de los Reyes, a most unusual and very interesting piece of graffiti. He had spent every day since looking for similar examples and analysing them. He got out his papers and showed Moya his drawings. The ginger cat had jumped onto the desk and was rubbing its head against Souto's hand.

'Stop it, Derri,' he said and began to explain the sign's characteristics. 'It's composed of two concentric circles that are usually broken at two points. I've followed the trail and found that the sign is repeated in almost all the stations on Line 2, near the exits, at about three and a half feet from the floor. I'll show you.'

On his insistence, Moya had to accompany him to the station. The entrance in Calle de los Reyes was closed, so they went to the exit on the corner of Calle de Noviciado. When they reached the entrance, Souto indicated a kind of round, matt black stain, which stood out against the tiles on the wall.

'There it is,' said Souto. He moved closer and sniffed the sign, then touched it gently with his fingertips. 'It smells faintly of amber and has a velvety texture, although I've found that this depends on the type of wall, because it doesn't smell or feel the same on concrete as it does on stone. What do you think?'

Moya shrugged, because he could see nothing unusual about the mark, which seemed to him yet another mani-festation of the selfish behaviour of certain antisocial individuals. Then, lowering his voice as if to confide a secret, Souto added:

'It wasn't applied with a spray gun, I've checked, it's as if it had been stamped on.'

His search for these signs and others like them kept Souto busy all that autumn, and he got used to consider-ing the office not only his bedroom, but also his study and the centre of his investigations. In the local area, people knew him as The Poet, because that is how Moya had described him, rather than as a professor, when he intro-duced him to the porter, telling him that the gentleman was at liberty to come and go as he pleased. Souto also proved to be a precise and attentive minder of the cats, to whom he even gave names.

In a conversation he had with Souto towards the end of December, Moya learned that the stubborn professor had an almost obsessive interest in those circular signs. Most graffiti, he believed, were the expression of one individual, whose principal aim was that his marks should be seen by other people. However, the circular signs seemed to him to contain a message addressed to a particular recipient and with a particular end in mind.

Moya thought him over-excited. Sometimes he brought him something to eat, because he suspected that Souto often went without food for long periods, leaving untouched the money Moya occasionally left for him on the desk. Eventually, Souto explained that he didn't need food, because he shared the cats' supper.

'What's good for one mammal should be good enough for me, especially as I need so little,' he argued.

Moya began to fear that Souto's long periods of abstinence were beginning to affect his intellectual faculties.

'Do you know what a mandala is?' Souto asked him, once again spreading out on the flat surfaces in the office the pieces of paper on which he had reproduced the numerous circular signs he had come across on Line 2 of the metro. 'A mandala is a window that opens at the point where the disparate and the unitary, the confused and the clear, the imaginary and the real all meet.' He looked up and there was in his eyes a look of triumph, a kind of solemn joy. 'These signs are the heart of the lotus flower, the centre of a mandala that someone is printing on the walls, although quite how I don't know. I intend to penetrate their deeper meaning and find out who is sending the message and who is receiving it. I already have a lot of data.'

One morning, a few days later, Moya went down the steep steps into the office and found Souto standing to attention in the middle of the room, staring fixedly up at the ceiling, with the cat he called Derri perched on his shoulders.

'Professor Souto,' cried Moya, 'whatever's wrong?'

Souto took a few seconds to emerge from his motionless trance, but when he did, he was extraordinarily animated.

'My friend,' he replied, 'I've discovered that I myself am the person for whom the message is intended.'

Moya sat down in his rickety chair and stared at Professor Souto in some concern. Souto maintained his stiff, almost arrogant pose. The ginger cat was walking back and forth on his shoulders and rubbing his head against Souto's beard. Souto, calmer now, continued talking.

'A few days ago, at about three o'clock in the morning, I was woken by the phone ringing, but at the other end, all I could hear was a meaningless murmur, a kind of guttural gurgling. I was inclined to think that someone had simply dialled the wrong number, but the suspicion grew inside me that it might well be a message that I was unable to understand. It happened again the following day and I heard the same gurglings, a barely articulated sound that clearly wasn't coming from any electronic source. Finally, tonight, I understood.'

Souto gently picked up the cat with both hands, removed it from his shoulders, and set it down on the ground. Then he stood up and asked Moya the time.

'It's ten twenty-five,' said Moya, 'but finish telling me what happened last night. Don't leave me in suspense.'

Souto pointed a finger at him and said in an admonitory tone:

'So you want to know, do you? Well, come with me to the skip in Calle de Silva and I'll tell you on the way.'

Then, spreading wide his arms, like a tenor about to launch into a romantic song, he let out a long, resonant sound.

It was very cold, and Moya wrapped his scarf tightly about his neck. Souto did not speak again until they reached Calle de la Luna. As they walked up the street, Souto, panting a little with the effort, continued his story. His breath emerged from his mouth in clouds of vapour.

'You probably don't know what the first mantra is either, the one that contains the breath of life. Well, the phone rang again and, although I don't wear a watch, I reckon it must have been just before dawn. I expected to hear the same guttural noises as before, but this time I clearly heard the sound of the first mantra. Before they hung up, it was repeated five times, ooommm, ooommm, five times.'

The skip in Calle de Silva contained only some discarded broken window frames and a dilapidated bed base, but Souto did not seem in the least put out.

'Some early birds must have got here before us. When you live on the street, you have to be very quick,' he said philosophically, then asked Moya to buy him a coffee.

'The first mantra. Do you understand? I immediately sensed that this was a message that connected up with all the guttural gurglings of the previous days, and I felt sure there was a connection, too, between that sound message and the circular sign. I thought, and fortunately I was right, that someone was at last beginning to make the sign comprehensible to me. My tireless search for those circular signs had been a kind of acknowledgement of receipt, the blind response that someone was waiting for, and, at last, they had found me, because the circular sign that had first attracted my attention was placed there precisely for that reason, and my interest had attracted the notice of the messengers. After all, is not every individual, at every moment, a sign that must combine with other signs in order to achieve universal harmony? And do not all our ills come from the lack of balance and harmony between the signs that we represent?'

'Are you sure you don't want something to eat? Some *churros* perhaps or a sandwich,' Moya said.

'Man does not live by bread alone, Moya, so don't be such a pest. Don't you realize that I am close to finding the one truth of my life? I know now that I am a sign and that I have awoken in some mysterious being the same desire to decipher me that I felt when I found those rough, irregular concentric circles.'

It must have been about four o'clock in the morning, the moment of greatest silence, after most of the night rubbish collections have been made and before the first cars of the day have begun to stir, when the phone rang in Moya's apartment. He woke with a start and rushed to answer it.

'What's wrong?' asked his wife, somewhat alarmed.

'Oh, nothing serious, but I need to go and make sure. It's Souto, that friend of mine who sleeps at the office. He was saying some very strange things.'

'I'm phoning to say goodbye,' Souto had said. 'I've spoken to the people of the sign. They've just told me that they're coming to pick me up. It will be a very long journey, which means that you and I won't see each other again.'

What can one do in the face of such obsession, Moya was thinking as he drove through the deserted city. He'll end up dying in the street of starvation or pneumonia, in the grip of his delirium, and that will be that. He parked the car opposite the alleyway and, just as he was going round the corner, saw Souto leaving the office, carrying the ginger cat in his arms.

'Souto, wait,' he called and quickened his pace.

Souto stopped in the middle of the street and stood looking at him with what was clearly a smile of farewell on his face, the final gesture of someone about to take his leave.

When he was only about five paces away from Souto, Moya bumped into an invisible barrier that prevented him from going any further. That invisible barrier was not entirely rigid to the touch, and so the collision had not been a painful one, but it was as if the air had suddenly taken on a density similar to that of a solid body, and it was impossible to get any closer to the professor.

'Souto, what's going on, what's happened?'

'Goodbye, friend Moya, my kindly publisher. I have found my sign and I hope that, one day, you will find yours. Now, remember, don't even think about reprinting my poems, and thank you for everything. I'm taking Derri with me. I'll take good care of him.'

Moya's growing amazement left him paralysed and powerless until daybreak, as he watched the area around the spot where Souto was standing grow steadily more opaque until Souto was completely hidden from view and was replaced by a great white block that grew darker and darker until it was a huge, long, hazy shape. Moya tried to touch that compact mass, but the invisible deterrent prevented him from doing so. Then the great oblong cloud moved slowly over to the building opposite his office, gradually becoming embedded in the wall there and, finally, disappearing altogether, leaving the street empty.

On the wall into which the vast nebulous parallelepiped had vanished was a large piece of graffiti, a black sign that seemed to represent two capital letters, an upside-down Y, with a U superimposed on the upper part of the vertical stroke, forming a trident with a forked handle. Above the sign was another smaller one rather like a tilde, except that one end was much thicker than the other. Moya went over to the wall and gingerly reached out one hand to touch it: the marks were slightly raised and still warm.

When he finally got home and into bed, gripped by a trembling that his wife attributed to the effects of standing out in the damp morning air, Moya was thinking that the absurd events he believed he had witnessed probably belonged merely to the nonsense realm of dreams. But when he returned to the office two days later, he discovered that the sign was still there on the wall, despite all the porters' attempts to remove it. The sign remained, and Moya regarded it with a mixture of sorrow and wonder, because he knew that it was the only trace left of Souto, after his astonishing disappearance.

One day, when he went into the metro station nearest his house, he saw that on the wall in the entrance, a workman was painting a circular shape similar to those that had filled Professor Souto's final studies and obsessions.

'What are you doing?' asked Moya.

The man made another irregular circle, then put the brush back in the large paint pot slung over his arm.

'We're marking the spot where the fire hydrant should go,' he said. 'They're installing them in every station.'

Notes on the Authors

1. **Benito Pérez Galdós** (1843–1920) is considered to be Spain's greatest nineteenth-century novelist, on a par with Dickens and Balzac. Born in the Canary Islands, he moved to Madrid when he was 19 and spent most of his adult life there. He wrote novels, plays, and stories, his masterpiece being *Fortunata y Jacinta*. Although his work is usually described as Realist, there is often an element of the fantastic in his writing (as in this story) and this was perhaps what attracted the film-maker Luis Buñuel, who based three of his films on Galdós novels: *Viridiana*, *Nazarín*, and *Tristana*.

2. **Emilia Pardo Bazán** (1851–1921) was born in A Coruña in Galicia, and many of her novels are set in that region. She married at 16 and moved with her husband to Madrid, where she lived until her death. She was a prolific writer and is often credited with introducing Naturalism into Spanish literature. Her most famous work is *Los Pazos de Ulloa*. She and Galdós became

lovers for a time and remained friends throughout their lives. She took a keen interest in politics and played an important role in the development of the feminist movement in Spain.

3. **Alonso Zamora Vicente** (1916–2006) was a philologist, lexiocographer, dialectologist, and writer. Born in Madrid, his studies were interrupted by the Civil War, but he completed his degree in 1940 and went on to teach at all the major universities in Spain and was visiting professor at many others in Latin America, America, and Europe. He founded various journals and magazines and was a prolific writer of short stories. This story comes from *Primeras hojas*, published in 1985, which contains a series of evocative descriptions of the Madrid of his childhood.

4. **Juan García Hortelano** (1928–92) was born in Madrid and spent the years of the Civil War between Cuenca and Madrid. He was very much an autodidact and prided himself on combining his writing with his job as a civil servant in Madrid. He wrote short stories, novels, and poetry and also translated such writers as Robert Walser, Céline, and Boris Vian.

5. **Guillermo Busutil** (b. 1961) was born in Granada and is still based in Andalusia. He has published several

collections of short stories and won numerous prizes. He has also worked as a journalist, commentator, and presenter on radio and television.

6. **Álvaro Pombo** (b. 1939) was born in Santander and studied in Madrid and at Birkbeck College, London, where he lived for eleven years. A resident of Madrid since then, he writes poetry, short stories, and novels, two of which have been translated into English as *The Hero of the Big House* and *The Resemblance*. He won the 2006 Premio Planeta with his novel *La Fortuna de Matilda Turpin*.

7. **Ignacio Aldecoa** (1925–69) was born in Vitoria, but lived in Madrid for most of his adult life. He was part of a group of writers who began to publish in the late 1940s, a group that included Rafael Sánchez Ferlosio, Carmen Martín Gaite, and Jesús Fernández Santos. He wrote novels and short stories. His novel *Gran Sol* won the 1958 Premio de la Crítica.

8. **Carmen Martín Gaite** (1925–2000) was born in Salamanca, but lived most of her adult life in Madrid. She was one of Spain's foremost women writers, and her work has been widely translated (*Variable Cloud, The Farewell Angel*, and *The Back Room* are available in English). She wrote poetry, novels, short stories, plays,

and children's fiction, as well as essays on a variety of subjects. She also worked as a translator, translating such works as *Wuthering Heights* and *Madame Bovary*. She was married to fellow writer Rafael Sánchez Ferlosio.

9. **Medardo Fraile** (b. 1925) was born in Madrid, but since 1964 has lived in Scotland, where he was Professor of Spanish at the University of Strathclyde until his retirement. As a student he was very involved in the theatre, but abandoned that to devote himself to writing. He specializes in short stories that take their inspiration from the ordinary lives of ordinary people. He has won various prizes, notably the Premio Nacional de la Crítica.

10. **Jorge Ferrer-Vidal** (1926–2001) was born in Barcelona, but his family fled the city in 1936, with the outbreak of civil war. They returned when the war was over, and he studied law at Barcelona University, only moving to Madrid during the latter part of his life. He wrote novels and poetry, as well as working as a literary translator, but his favourite genre was always the short story.

11. **Marina Mayoral** (b. 1942) was born in Mondoñedo in Galicia, and writes in Galician and Spanish. She taught

Spanish Literature at the Complutense University in Madrid until her retirement. She writes short stories and novels, and since 1990, has written a weekly column in *Voz de Galicia.*

12. **Carlos Castán** (b. 1960) was born in Barcelona, graduated in Philosophy from the Universidad Autónoma in Madrid, and currently teaches at a secondary school in Zaragoza. He has always specialized in the short story and these have appeared in many literary reviews and anthologies in Spain.

13. **Eloy Tizón** (b. 1964) was born in Madrid and has written novels and short stories. His novel *Seda salvaje* was shortlisted for the XIII Premio Herralde, and his story collection *Velocidad de los jardines* (Anagrama, 1992) was chosen by the critics of *El País* as one of the hundred most interesting books in Spanish of the last twenty-five years. Alejandro Cánovas made a short film based on *Flying Fish* (see: http://vimeo.com/3319797).

14. **José Ferrer-Bermejo** (1956–2003) was born in Alcalá de Henares. He began three different degrees, but finished none of them. He worked as a postman in Madrid, and began his literary career with a collection of short stories, *El increíble hombre inapetente y otros relatos.* He also wrote four novels.

15. Javier Marías (b. 1951) was born in Madrid, where he still lives. He spent part of his childhood in America, where his father, the philosopher Julián Marías, held various teaching posts. He also taught for two years at Oxford University. He is widely considered to be Spain's foremost contemporary novelist and has won almost every literary prize going, apart from the Nobel. He has also translated such writers as Laurence Sterne, Nabokov, Faulkner, and Sir Thomas Browne.

16. Juan José Millás (b. 1946) was born in Valencia, but moved with his family to Madrid in 1952. He worked in a bank and then for Iberia, writing short stories and novels in his spare time. Since winning the Premio Sésamo with his second novel, *Cerbero son las sombras*, he has written ten novels, several collections of short stories, and contributes a weekly column to *El País*. Since then, he has won many other prizes, among them, the Premio Planeta and the Premio Nacional de Narrativa.

17. Carmen Posadas (b. 1953) was born in Montevideo, Uruguay, but has lived in Madrid since 1965 and has Spanish nationality. She began her literary career in 1980 writing books for children. In 1984, she won the Premio Nacional de Literatura (Spanish literature prize), then moved into adult fiction, winning the

1998 Premio Planeta with her second novel *Pequeñas infamias*. Her books have sold more than a million copies in more than fifty countries and she has been translated into twenty-one languages.

18. **Elvira Lindo** (b. 1962) was born in Cádiz, but moved to Madrid when she was 12. She began working in television and radio, and her first novel was based on one of her fictional radio characters, Manolito Gafotas, the son of a truck-driver, who lives in the working-class district of Carabanchel. Manolito has since become a classic of Spanish children's literature. She is married to fellow writer Antonio Muñoz Molina.

19. **José María Merino** (b. 1941) was born in A Coruña, Galicia. He lived for several years in León and currently lives in Madrid. He is a master of the short story, and has a particular penchant for the fantastic. He is also a poet, novelist, children's writer, and travel writer and a teacher of creative writing. His work has brought him various prizes, including the Premio Nacional de la Crítica.

Further Reading

Apart from the usual excellent guidebooks to Madrid—DK Eyewitness, Lonely Planet, Time Out, Blue Guide, etc., I would recommend the following, which look at Madrid from a more literary and historical angle:

Madrid Observed by Michael Jacobs (Pallas Athene, 1992) offers seven thematically based walks through the history of Madrid. Includes detailed maps, historical illustrations, full index, and practical information. It also has a useful list of books about Madrid.

A Traveller's Companion to Madrid, introduced and edited by Hugh Thomas (Constable & Robinson Ltd, 2008) contains selections from diaries, letters, memoirs, and novels ranging across five centuries of Madrid's history. It also has an excellent bibliography.

Madrid: A Cultural and Literary History by Elizabeth Nash (Signal Books, 2006) is a fascinating guide to the history of Madrid and the artists and writers it has produced.

A Handbook for Travellers in Spain, Part II by Richard Ford (1896) is the classic traveller's guide to Spain. Part II includes his comments on Madrid. Not easy to come by, but worth hunting down on the Internet.

Spain: A Literary Companion by Jimmy Burns (Santana Books, n.d.) has a good chapter on Madrid as seen by various foreign visitors.

Diccionario de Madrid (Las calles, sus nombres, su historia, su ambiente) by Antonio Cabezas (Avapies, 1989) is the definitive guide (in Spanish) to Madrid's streets and history.

My Last Breath by Luis Buñuel (translated by Abigail Israel; Vintage, 1994). Buñuel's autobiography, includes a vivid picture of his time in Madrid (chapter 7) at the Resi—the Residencia de los Estudiantes—where he was friends with Federico García Lorca and Salvador Dalí.

The Forging of a Rebel by Arturo Barea (translated by Ilsa Barea; Spanish edition first published in 3 volumes in 1941, 1943, and 1946; omnibus edition published by Walker & Co., New York, 2001). Barea was born into a poor family in Madrid in 1897. He provides vivid descriptions of the slums, beggars, and children of the city he knew as a child and, in volume III, *The Clash*, chronicles the events in Madrid during the Spanish Civil War. A literary and historical masterpiece.

Novels set in Madrid (and available in English)

Arturo Pérez-Reverte's Captain Alatriste novels: *Captain Alatriste* and *The Purity of Blood* (translated by Margaret Sayers Peden); *The King's Gold* and *The Man in the Yellow Doublet* (translated by Margaret Jull Costa); all published by Weidenfeld & Nicolson. These swashbuckling novels give a vivid picture of seventeenth-century Madrid.

Fortunata and Jacinta by Benito Pérez Galdós (first published 1886; translated by Agnes Moncy Gullón; Penguin Classics, 1988). Galdós's masterpiece, and one of the greatest novels to come out of Spain.

The Maravillas District by Rosa Chacel (first published 1976; translated by D. A. Demers; University of Nebraska Press, 1992). This autobiographical novel follows the lives of two young women growing up in turn-of-the-century Madrid.

Winter in Madrid by C. J. Sansom (Macmillan, 2006). A meticulously researched novel set in Madrid in 1940, just after the Spanish Civil War ended.

The Hive by Camilo José Cela (first published 1953; translated by J. M. Cohen and Arturo Barea; Dalkey Archive Press, 2001). Considered to be the Nobel Laureate's masterpiece, the book details the lives of 300 characters living in the slums of Madrid.

The River by Rafael Sánchez Ferlosio (first published 1955; translated by Margaret Jull Costa; Dedalus, 2004). In this novel set on a hot summer's day by the river Jarama, Sánchez Ferlosio brilliantly summons up both the pleasures of a day out and the narrowness and tedium of life in 1950s Madrid.

Time of Silence by Luis Martín-Santos (first published 1962, although an uncensored version was not published until 1982; translated by George Leeson; Columbia University Press, 1989). Set in the early 1950s, this is another searing indictment of Franco's Spain.

The Patty Diphusa Stories and Other Writings by Pedro Almodóvar (translated by Kirk Anderson; Faber & Faber, 1992). Insubstantial titbits evocative of the whole *movida* era.

A Heart So White and *Tomorrow in the Battle Think On Me* by Javier Marías (translated by Margaret Jull Costa; Harvill 1995 and 1996). Both these novels are set largely in Madrid and capture, as only Marías can, the darker side of life in the city.

Short-story collections

Most short-story collections of 'Spanish' stories tend to concentrate on Latin American writers. I give below two

Medardo Fraile—Ojos inquietos
From: *Cuentos de verdad*, Editora Nacional, 1964

Jorge Ferrer-Vidal—Mozart, K. 124, para flauta y orquesta
From: *El cuento español 1940–1980*, Castalia didáctica, 1989

Marina Mayoral—A través del tabique
From: *Morir en tus brazos y otros cuentos*, Aguaclara, 1989

Carlos Castán—Viaje de regreso
From: *Museo de la Soledad*, Tropo Editores, 2007

Eloy Tizón—Pez volador
From: *Parpadeos*, Anagrama, 2006

José Ferrer-Bermejo—Dejen salir
From: *Incidente en Atocha*, Alfaguara, 1982

Javier Marías—Caídos en desgracia
From: *El País*, August 2005

Juan José Millás—Trastornos de carácter
From: *Primavera de luto*, Destino, 1989

Carmen Posada - ¿Cómo puede pasarme esto a mí?
From: *Literatura, adulterio una Visa platino*, Planeta, 2007

Elvira Lindo—El cuerno de Manolito
From: *Manolito Gafotas*, Santillana, 2000

José María Merino—Signo y mensaje
From: *Cuentos*, Castalia didáctica, 2000

Calle de Serrano

Calle de las Pozas

Calle de Noviciado

Calle Alberto Aguilera

Argüelles Ⓜ

Calle de la Princesa

Ventura Ⓜ Rodriguez

Buen Suceso

Avenida Complutense

Glorieta de San

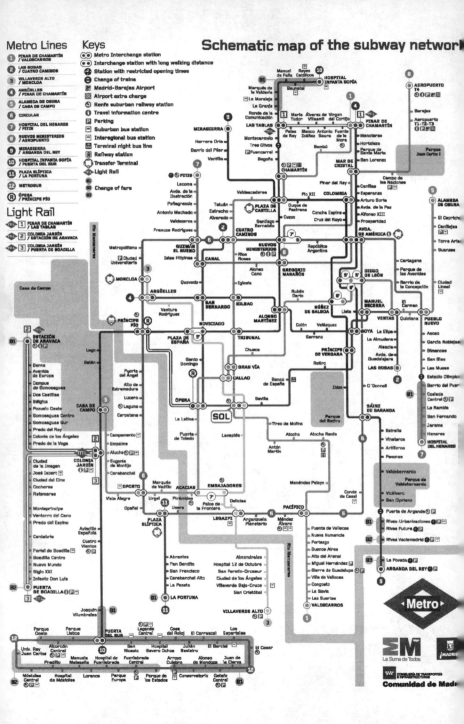